# DOUBLE EXPOSURE

# DOUBLE EXPOSURE

## BRIDGET BIRDSALL

**Sky Pony Press**

NEW YORK

Sky Pony Press books may be purchased in bulk at special discounts for sales promotion, corporate gifts, fund-raising, or educational purposes. Special editions can also be created to specifications. For details, contact the Special Sales Department, Sky Pony Press, 307 West 36th Street, 11th Floor, New York, NY 10018 or info@skyhorsepublishing.com.

Sky Pony® is a registered trademark of Skyhorse Publishing, Inc.®, a Delaware corporation.

Visit our website at www.skyponypress.com.

10 9 8 7 6 5 4 3 2 1

Library of Congress Cataloging-in-Publication Data

Birdsall, Bridget.
Double exposure / Bridget Birdsall.
pages cm
Summary: Fifteen-year-old Alyx Atlas starts school in a new state with a new identity–as a girl–but a bully on the basketball court threatens to reveal that Alyx is an intersex person, which could disqualify Alyx and the team from playing in the state championship game.
ISBN 978-1-62914-606-5 (hardback)
[1. Intersex people–Fiction. 2. Gender identity–Fiction. 3. Bullying–Fiction. 4. High schools–Fiction. 5. Schools–Fiction. 6. Basketball–Fiction. 7. Moving, Household–Fiction.] I. Title.
PZ7.B511965Dou 2014
[Fic]–dc23
2014015992

Cover design by Jaime Heiden and Brian Peterson
Cover art credit Jaime Heiden

Ebook ISBN: 978-1-63220-206-2

Printed in the United States of America

## Dedication

*For Jeffrey and those who have been judged or bullied for being different. In the game of life there will be times you will want to give up—don't.*
*Stay in the game. The world needs you more than ever.*

*And in memory of Nancy Garden, who believed in this book from the beginning.*

# DOUBLE EXPOSURE

# CHAPTER 1

# Prickman

Living in the Valley was like being hunted every day of my life.

Either you fit in or you didn't. There were no gray areas at Walnut Grove High. If you were different, they'd sniff you out, track you down. You had two options: stand and fight, or run like hell. After Dad died, I guess I just got sick of running.

Now Prickman and his apes are three thousand miles away, but my brain keeps taking random trips back in time, dragging my body along with it, and suddenly, I'm there—pushing through the grime-streaked doors of the 7-Eleven, Dad's basketball in one hand and an icy can of root beer in the other. Hot valley air slapping my face, making me ache for the California coast.

"Hey, Pretty-boy!" Ricky Pearlman, a senior everyone calls Prickman, barks at me from across the parking lot. He and his Neanderthals are fussing with someone's bicycle. Stolen, no doubt.

I pop the top off my root beer, tuck Dad's ball under one arm, and turn toward the back of the building, hoping Rafi, the owner, is watching from inside the store, but all I see is the reflection of my own lanky body. The baggy shirt that hides my budding breasts makes me look like some strange hybrid between a pregnant giraffe and a praying mantis. And I'm wishing I'd pulled my socks up higher because, though I'd look like a complete moron, perhaps I wouldn't have to defend my shaved legs again.

"At-*ass*, I'm talkin' to *you*!"

I try to ignore him.

It had worked before.

"Wait up, faggot!"

No such luck.

He heads my way, and I pick up my pace. Root beer splashes over my fingers, and I take a quick sip hoping not to spill more. He stomps up onto the sidewalk blocking my path. I stop, hold the can up like an offering.

"You can call me Alyx. Want some?"

He eyes me suspiciously, pushing my arm away. "Don't like pussies ignorin' me." His freshly shaved head shines in the afternoon sunlight. He reeks of sweat and stale cigarettes. Muscles bulge up under his shirtsleeves, putting my skinny arms to shame.

"Okay, then," I say, roll my eyes, smile, and carefully step around him. "Sorry, can't stay and chat, gotta go." I try not to look scared. I'd learned from experience once guys like Prickman sense you're scared, it's over.

Then I decide to make a dash for it, but when I round the corner, his tough-guy buddies are waiting.

"Did ya miss us?"

They surround me, and I freeze. An old familiar panic pushes into my throat.

Prickman glances back. No one is around, and I've managed to get myself into a fairly isolated spot, hemmed in with hedges and traffic noise, out of view from the front sidewalk. My legs begin to tremble so hard I'm afraid I might pee myself.

"What you doin' at our store, anyway? Didn't we warn you already?" Prickman's Adam's apple sticks out like a broken bone.

My heart's doing double-time. Gulping down panic, I pretend to look around. "Didn't see your name on it, unless," I shrug, sounding tougher than I feel, "you changed it to *7- Eleven* and forgot to tell me?"

Now why I say stuff like this I'll never know.

A slow smile spreads across Prickman's mangy face. "Think you're real smart, don't you? A real val-e-*dick*-torian? Huh — *At-ass*."

I don't bother to tell him my last name is pronounced *Atlas*, as in the *World Atlas*. Instead, I turn to run, but he shoves me from behind, and in a whirlwind of root beer, I slam down onto the blacktop, my arms shooting out to break the fall, a cracking sound echoing in my ears. My phone? My hipbone?

Prickman catches Dad's ball on a bounce, spins, does a jump shot into the dumpster. "Three points!" he cries, and they all laugh.

My knees are on fire.

"Make 'em fight!" The one with a six-pack rippling under his skintight Nike T-shirt sneers at me.

I brush off embedded gravel, grit my teeth, knowing better than to cry.

"He looks like a girl. He sounds like a girl. Let's see if he fights like one, too." Prickman nudges his ratty boot against my crotch. I try to scoot away, get back up, but he presses harder.

"Make 'im fight, let's see 'im fight." Mr. Nike T-shirt won't shut up.

Surprising even myself, I spring to my feet and, swinging wildly, fly at Prickman. Warm rivulets of blood drip down my legs as my fists hit only air, but I don't care, because this time, if I'm going down, I'm going down fighting.

Prickman dances out of the way, laughing, "Oooo, I'm sooo scared."

They start ping-ponging my body from one to the other, while Mr. Nike-man stomps on my shoelace, trapping my left foot as a searing pain rips through my leg. I wince and push myself off Prickman, who has me firmly by the shorts, ready to deliver one of his famous Walnut Grove wedgies. Kicking at him with my free foot, I scramble from his grip and regain my balance when suddenly, without warning, he tightens his hold, and instead of yanking up, he yanks down. Pulling my jersey shorts along with a brand new pair of hot-pink bikini briefs straight down to my knees.

Time stops. They stare. My legs give way.

"H-o-l-y s-h-i-t!" is all I hear before planting face first onto the pavement.

CHAPTER 2

# The Polish Palace

Change is good, right?

Dad used to say that change is the only real constant, but that was then; this is now. And now, we're talkin' mega change, a move across the country. New home. New school. New identity. Milwaukee, Wisconsin. It smells worse than LA smog. I plug my nose as Mom shifts into third and we cross the Harbor Street Bridge. Mom points out the window below to dozens of church steeples, smokestacks, and snaky black waterways.

I can't tell where she's pointing.

All I know is Grandpa and Uncle Grizzly live somewhere on Milwaukee's South Side; this is her old stomping ground, not mine.

"Usinger's Sausage factory!" She smiles. Her graying Rasta braids whip in the wind.

I nod. I'd have preferred to start high school on the California coast, but after the 7-Eleven incident, I agreed to move anywhere, even Milwaukee-in-the-middle-of-nowhereville, as long as I can be who I really am.

5

I lick my lips. The taste of blood mixes with watermelon lipgloss. I duck down so Mom won't see. She'll have a meltdown if she sees blood on my face. I can't handle that right now. Unplugging my nose, I rummage under the seat for a water bottle. Carefully wipe at my mouth before I pop back up.

My hip still has a weird twinge in it, and I stifle a groan as the memory of Prickman's butt-ugly face flashes in front of mine.

Halfway across the country and he's still haunting me.

Wishing I could torch that memory plug, I flip down the visor to check the scrape on my cheek. It's healed and my lip would be, too, if I'd stop chomping on it.

"You okay?" Mom looks at me as she pulls the Sunbug up in front of the Polish Palace, a house that, until now, I've only seen in photos.

I nod.

She slams the stick into park. "Ready?"

She sounds as scared as I feel.

I make myself suck in a deep breath and wipe my hands, sticky with sweat, across the thighs of my new jeans. No time to worry if my new pearlescent nail polish matches my tank top. "Ready as I'll ever be."

With Dad gone, I try to sound strong, for her sake.

On the peeling porch of the Polish Palace, Grizzly waves his beefy hand and pushes himself off a swing that bends dangerously in the middle. He says something to Grandpa, who's sitting in a rickety rocker. The traffic noise drowns out every sound, except the *bhonk, bhonk, bhonk* of a basketball at the park across the street.

The sound calms me.

A girl about my age with flame-red hair, wearing a Tennessee jersey, sinks a three-pointer. The ball clangs through the chain-link net, making my fingers fidget, and my legs want to take off in a fast break—

"Hey, Sis!" Grizzly bellows.

I force myself to focus. Mammoth, my uncle's leather-clad form lumbers down to greet us. Part of the porch rail has fallen off, and it's lying in a patch of un-mowed grass. Next to it is a motorcycle graveyard. The neighboring houses are big and boxy, too, and there's a white mansion on the other side of the park that looks strangely out of place.

Mom jumps out and runs to hug him. He practically picks her up off the ground.

"You made it. I was startin' to worry."

His fingers and forearms are stained with tattoos and beads of sweat pop out on his forehead. Shoulder-length, almost-white blond hair blows wildly in the wind. Thank God, it's the only Kowalski trait I seem to have inherited.

"Wait'll you see . . . freshly painted . . . Alyx's room is set." He sounds breathless. There's a splotch of lavender paint on his T-shirt.

"She'll love it," Mom says, in her eternally positive sunshine way, stressing the "she" part, which probably isn't needed. She's been lecturing them on the phone practically every night for the last two weeks.

Grizzly sets Mom down. He waves and calls shyly, "Hey, Alyx."

"Hi, Uncle Joe," I say through the open window, wondering if he and Grandpa will act like nothing is up. Like I've always been this way—just a regular girl.

Grandpa starts to roust himself from the rocker, but Grizzly shouts, "Stay put, Pops! We're comin' to you."

Mom opens the passenger door.

"Ready or not." She smiles down at me.

My heart joins my stomach, doing push-ups against the inside cavity of my chest wall, and my new jog bra suddenly feels like it shrunk two sizes. Worst of all, our little family reunion has attracted the attention of the redhead, who's stopped shooting to stare. She whips a phone from her sock and starts texting.

Great. I don't let myself think about *who* she's telling *what*, and I'm way too busy fending off a heart attack to notice the pit hollowing itself out in my belly. I hate when people stare, especially when they stare at me. It makes me feel like a freak.

Mom reaches for my hand. "Come on, Honey. Remember, fresh start, right?"

# CHAPTER 3

# Super Freak

Fresh start. Our new code words. A direct result of my run-in with Prickman and his apes. At first, Mom wanted to do it the old way—try to convince me that we should report them.

"Alyx, you have every right to be safe here." She didn't get that it wasn't personal with Prickman. He sensed I was different, and that's what guys like him do; sniff out and hunt down super-freaks.

"It's not just Ricky Pearlman and his dweebs, Mom. You don't get it, do you?" I'd told her.

"What's that supposed to mean?"

"Doesn't matter."

"Yes, it does. Alyx, for God's sake, it matters to me. You matter to me!" Both she and I knew I couldn't survive another beating. Her guilt was palpable. "Your dad and I did the best we could."

"It's not that—"

"If you'd just talk to me, Alyx."

"I tell you everything, Mom!" Hot with rage, I'd whipped off the T-shirt I'd slept in. "LOOK!"

She blushed, but she didn't look away. I laid my hands over my small, but obviously budding breasts, tried to get her to see. "Ricky and his buddies are growing beards, and I'm growing these. What do you expect them to do? I'm a friggin' freak!"

"You are not a freak, Alyx."

"Yeah? Then what am I?"

"I will not allow you to denigrate yourself like this."

"I told you. I told Dad. I showed you guys. I tried telling you a long time ago, but you wouldn't listen."

"We did listen, Alyx. We didn't want to overreact and regret things later. That's why we found Dr. Max. So you would have someone to talk to."

"Yeah, then Dad conveniently got cancer because he couldn't deal with the fact that you guys screwed up. Got him out of family therapy for life—right?"

"No one screwed up."

"You did! Majorly. I'm living proof."

"STOP IT!"

I scrambled into the corner, yanked my shirt back on, and glared at her.

"Why didn't you just make me a girl? That's what everyone else does with their ambiguous babies, right?"

"Alyx, you know it's not as simple as a DNA test. If it was, we'd have done it."

"Dad would've rather had half-a-boy than a whole girl, right?"

"That's not true."

"It is. He told me."

"We didn't want to choose for you. That's what he told you." She put her head in her hands. "We wanted you to lead the way."

She started to cry. I wanted her to feel bad, but after a few minutes, I got up, went over, and touched her shoulder.

"Mom?" I said. "You want to know how I feel?"

She nodded. She was sitting on the edge of the bed, her face still in her hands.

"Like I'm stuck with your mistake. And I can't do it anymore. I can't be a boy. Not for you. Not for Dad. Not for anyone." My voice got all shaky. "Because, I'm a girl. I always have been. And now Dad's gone, so we both need to face the facts." I sank down to my knees in front of her.

"Genetically you're—"

"Neither! Both! I know! Intersex. Eunuch. Hermaphrodite. Ambiguous genitalia! One of the two percent of twenty-one mutant genderless baby strains born every year, and none of that matters, because you know what, Mom? I still need to pick a Goddamn locker room! That's why I want to be dead." The tears started streaming down my face. "Just like Dad. Dead. Dead. Dead." I hit my fist on the bed.

She grabbed me, hugged me, held me, and we both cried. Hard.

That's when she decided we were moving.

## CHAPTER 4

# Meat-Eating Fish

After Grizzly helps us haul up seven black plastic garbage bags crammed with clothes, Mom says, "Alyx, before you go out and play basketball, why don't you help Grizzly feed his fish?" It's her this-is-not-really-a-choice voice.

Carrying the ball Dad bequeathed to me, I follow Grizzly through the living room where Grandpa's taken out his hearing aid, set it on the lamp table, and fallen asleep sitting up. He's holding onto what looks like a huge set of knitting needles. A pearl-pedaled accordion leans up against his tattered La-Z-Boy. Super-thick glasses have slipped down his nose, and the sailboat pattern for a hook rug rests across his lap, which is dusted with little blue and white threads.

"Is he asleep?" I ask Grizzly, keeping my voice low.

"Yo, Pops, you out for the count?" Grizzly waves a handful of meat scraps in the air. "He must've tuckered himself out workin' on that rug."

When we reach the bottom step, Grizzly turns and whispers with a sly smile, "He'd be pissed if he knew I was feedin' my babies the good stuff."

"I heard that," Grandpa grumbles groggily from his chair.

"Course you did. When I need you to hear something, you conveniently go deaf." Grizzly giggles. It's an odd sound from such a huge man.

Stepping into the basement, I'm immediately grateful Mom and I are sleeping upstairs. Two bedroom doors along the far wall are cracked open, each revealing an unmade bed. The place smells damp and moldy, like a locker room. The ceilings are cracked, yellowed curtains hang on the squatty-windows, and rows and rows of buzzing florescent lights cast an eerie glow over dozens of vaporous fish tanks.

In the main area, there is not a single stick of furniture. Only fish tanks.

"You know, eleven of us Zuwalskis once lived in this basement?" Grizzly trundles up and down the aisles examining the fish. "Your great-grandpa hauled stone on horseback all the way from Chicago, built the basement first, lived here with all those kids 'til they could afford to build the house on top. Took ten years."

He reaches over and raps his knuckles against the wall. "Built 'em to last."

The tattooed letters splashed across his knuckles read: #1-F-A-T-B-O-Y-!

I pull Dad's basketball against my chest like it's some kind of shield. Secretly, I wish Grizzly had been with me that day with Prickman. Though he's obviously overweight, he still looks strong and scary, too.

Grizzly points from tank to tank.

"Here ya got your basic Treasure Island, thirty-six-g., with a classic sunken chest. Then, here's the Hawaiian Luau, only twenty-four-g., but the grass skirts are a neat effect, hey?"

Before I can reply, he continues, "In honor of your Grandma Clara, I found these guys with the Scottish kilts. And this one, she was my first—the Harley Haven."

"Cool fish-sized motorcycles," I say, hugging the basketball harder.

"Yeah," he smiles. "You ain't seen nothin'." He directs my attention to a gigantic tank neatly labeled with indelible marker: TANK OF TERROR. WARNING. CONTAINS MEAT-EATING FISH. Inside it, saucer-sized fish swarm in and out of a floating haunted house and a half-eaten mummy.

"For real?" I back away. Glad I'm not wearing flip-flops, in case I need to make a dash for it.

He nods and dumps a handful of meat scraps into the tank. The bronze-colored fish go wild. Leaping. Churning. Making a sick raspy, gasping sound. They devour the bloody mess in less than a minute.

"They love this stuff."

"What is it?" I stare. My stomach's churning.

"Pig brains, cow eyeballs. Stuff they can't use at the packing house."

"Cow eyeballs?"

No wonder Mom's a vegetarian. A sour lump rises in my throat.

"Here." Gently, he peels one of my hands from the basketball, and I slide the ball to my left hip as he slips me a slimy chunk. "Keep it at least six inches from the water," he warns. "These suckers can jump."

Who keeps a tank full of piranhas for pets?

It's like he hears what I'm thinking. "You ever had a pet?"

"A guinea pig. She died when I was seven."

He takes that in. It's been less than a year since Dad died, so he tries to steer the conversation elsewhere. "These fish'll teach you how predators think. Watch 'em a while. You'll see neither side's too far away from the other. Know what I mean?"

Not really, but I don't ask for clarity, just stand there mute.

"See, if you're being hunted, it helps to know how the hunter thinks." He guides my hand over the tank. "They use their instincts. They know what's coming. See?"

The fish begin to collide and churn, splashing water everywhere. I try to pull away, but holding tight Grizzly barks, "Let go," and I do.

The meat disappears in a whirlwind of water and bubbles.

"There ya go, darlin'. Nothin' to it."

He squeezes my hand and releases it. His hand is calloused, rough, damp, like a cat's tongue.

Suddenly, I feel sick. I can't tell if it's the dank air or the meat-eating fish or being called darlin'. But something deep inside of me rumbles like thunder, a terrible doubt. Like maybe I've gotten myself in over my head. Way over.

"You okay?" Grizzly snaps his finger against the basketball. "Hey, go out and play before you squeeze the air outta that thing!"

I turn and bound up the steps, two at a time.

## CHAPTER 5

# Daymares

I slam through the screen door and the mind-movie starts up again. I smell Prickman's ashtray stink and hear their voices, along with my own, sounding less than human, screaming: "LEAVE ME ALONE!"

What do you call it when nightmares come in the middle of the day? Daymares?

Part of me stands on the porch shaking; the other part is back there—again. Choking on blood, the sharp edges of my braces tearing the flesh inside my cheeks, my body folding in on itself. The convenience store door flying open and it's Rafi, the owner, with fear in his voice.

"You boys! I call police," he hollers in a thick East-Indian accent. "You boys. I tell you before—"

"What the hell is that?" Nike T-shirt stands over me, staring. "Shit! Run—towel-head!"

The pack scatters, their words lost in a trample of feet. "Jesus! See that? Did someone chop it off or what? He really is a girl."

I wipe my eyes in shame, and Rafi leans over me, holding a phone in one hand and a baseball bat in the other.

"Rafi, *no* police, please . . . call . . . Mom." I beg, trying not to swallow blood.

Rafi knows it's useless. He nods.

Five minutes later, Mom practically crash-lands in the parking lot. Mom—minus her sunshine smile. Her dented yellow Sunbug humming madly, her nurse's whites smelling of disinfectant and green apple shampoo, she leaps out and drops down beside me, her mother-bear eyes flashing.

"Did you call the police?" she demands of Rafi, not taking her eyes off me.

Rafi stands twitching under his silk kurta. His sandal-toed brown feet shuffle closer, and he points at me. "He say call you."

I'd managed to pull my shorts back up, but my hip hurt like hell. The new phone in my back pocket, now in pieces, pokes at my butt-cheek. Perfect! Mom warned a million times that if I toasted this one—that would be it. *It*—meaning no phone, period.

Given the circumstances, she'll spare me the lecture, her fingers expertly pressing the soft curve of my neck, her eyes searching mine for signs of dilation.

Satisfied—no concussion—she turns to Rafi. "Call now."

I shake my head, a wordless plea: *no, please, no!* She bites down on her lip. Our eyes lock—an invisible arch of lightning moves between us. Nothing new. This made the third time in less than a year we'd call the police. We needed another plan.

"It only makes it worse!" I argue.

"Alyx, what do you want me to do?" Desperation sounds in her voice.

"Please . . . don't make me hate you," I whisper, thinking about the last time Prickman and his pals took me down, peed on me. She didn't know, and I planned to keep it that way.

She gently pulls my head against her breast. Blood dripping from my nose spatters crimson specks onto her white uniform. She rocks me tenderly, fighting her own tears, not ready to let it go. "Alyx, who's responsible for this?"

"I call police, now?" Rafi points the bat in the direction where Prickman and his motley crew disappeared.

"NO!" I say forcefully, adding, "Mom, *listen* . . . we don't have to stay here anymore. Dad's gone. Let's get out of this place."

Her eyes well up, and she waves Rafi away. He shrugs his shoulders, turns, and pads back into the store.

Relieved, I close my eyes, letting the full weight of my head rest in her lap.

"*Who*, Alyx?" she demands, but she doesn't really want to know *who*; she doesn't. Over the years, I'd stopped talking about it. Silence. Mute. Moot point. Instinctively, I've always tried to protect her from the truth, the way she tries to protect me from the Prickmans of the world. We're both terrible liars.

I slap the ball between my hands, breaking the spell and looking across the street toward the park.

The redheaded girl's still out there shooting. That was then; this is now. I take off, leaping down the steps, the screen door banging shut behind me like a shotgun. The sound reverberates down the street. The girl stops, looks in my direction.

I push Prickman's ugly mug to the back of my brain, suck in the yeasty air, which feels like pure oxygen compared to the musty basement, force myself to smile, and run straight at her.

## CHAPTER 6

# The Pitmanis

As I cross the street to the basketball court, a hot gust brushes my face, rattling tree branches, scattering garbage. Already I'm sweating. Who knew Milwaukee in September could out-torch California's San Joaquin Valley?

Wiping my forehead with the sleeve of Dad's old T-shirt, I exhale and make myself keep going. Some guy with a camera has just joined the girl.

She stares, spits, and paws at the ground with her foot. She stops dribbling and watches me cross the street. The camera-guy turns his lens on me, clicking away, aiming first at my face and then at my feet.

I head straight for them, holding the ball in front of my face, until the camera gets too close for comfort and I duck behind a tree, not sure what to do next.

I hate having my picture taken!

"Peter—knock it off!" the girl hollers. She clamps her hand over the lens and shoves him roughly off the court.

"Aw, Pepper! Chill." He tugs the camera away.

"Sorry," she says as she walks toward me, rolling her eyes. Her face is speckled with freckles. "Stop acting like a weirdo!" she turns to the boy and punches his arm. She's pushing six-feet, almost as tall as me.

"Ow! Not everyone is anti-art," he explains. Dodging another blow, he smiles at me. "Are you?"

I stand cautiously behind the tree, staring at them.

The girl sighs. "My brother thinks everything he touches turns to art. Toilet paper rolls, french fries, a million still shots of people's shoes—"

He points at Dad's basketball. "You play?"

I nod.

"Praise Jesus!" He busts out laughing and does a little dance.

I smile. For the first time in weeks, my mouth isn't hurting.

He waves me toward him. He's shorter than her by a couple of inches, and unlike her fiery-green eyes, his are blue, like mine. A strange sensation shoots through me. Like I've met him someplace before. Though I know I haven't.

As if in a trance, I find myself walking again, straight toward him. He has jet-black hair. Cut short. The shadow of a day's beard covers his face. He's wearing faded jeans and a tennis jersey. Part of his collar is turned up in the back. Like he did it on purpose. Like it's a style thing.

He points at my T-shirt. "Where'd you get that?"

I stop. "My dad got his doctorate at Stanford. He was a huge fan."

"What changed?" Pushing his sister away, he flips the camera up to record my answer.

"He died."

"Oh." He lowers the camera. "Sorry."

The fact that Dad's dead is still sinking in.

"Peter, sometimes you're so dense." The girl shakes her head like we're on the same side against him. But I can tell he feels bad.

He puts out a hand. "I'm Peter."

I reach out and shake it, hoping mine's dry. His is warm, damp, and even though the gesture feels strange, it's comforting in an odd way.

The girl dribbles away from us. "Let her come shoot, Peter. Leave her alone."

"That's my sister, Patti," he steps toward me, lowers his voice. "It's spelled P-a-t-t-i. With an 'I' because it's all about her." He winks, releases my hand, then says in a normal tone, "Everyone calls her Pepper, because she's a total hothead." He ducks as a ball whizzes by his head.

"See," he whispers. "She takes medicine to help her moods."

"Give it a rest, okay?" Patti races by, picking the ball off the ground and calling over her shoulder, "Come shoot with me."

Peter steps out of my way. "Ladies first," he says, then whispers again. "Dad's pressuring her to get a basketball scholarship to Tennessee, his alma mater, so I'm trying to get her to lighten up in case she doesn't."

He grins. Without effort, I grin back. It feels like he's pulling me into some invisible force field and I have no power to resist. I look down and focus on my feet, which he now had about a hundred shots of. He zeroes his camera in on something under an oak tree and walks away, still talking. "Gotta go, can't quit my day job, but please, stay and play. Patti's relentless."

He spins around and looks back at me, "Hey, what's your name?"

"Alyx." I point at the Polish Palace. "Me and my mom just moved in." I don't point out that Alyx is spelled with a "yx" because my parents were trying to find a name that would fit. And I don't say my new last name, because taking on the whole *Kowalski* identity still feels totally foreign.

"You'll be going to Cudahy High?"

I nod.

"Cool!" He tips his head, smiles, and then begins walking in the direction of the white mansion on the other side of the park. When he reaches the street, he swings around looking through the camera lens, snaps a shot, and yells, "Make her work on fast breaks!"

"Shut up, Peter, let her play!" Pepper jogs over, and I catch the ball she tosses me with one hand, rolling Dad's onto the grass.

"Chillax, Sis." He laughs, turns, and takes off.

"You know the popcorn drill?" she asks, ignoring him, as I dribble over to join her.

Shaking my head, I pass the ball back, resisting the urge to glance back at him.

She takes off down the court, yelling, "Follow me!"

And I do.

# CHAPTER 7

# Deuce

The popcorn drill turns out to be the same one we used to warm up back in California. Only the guys I played with, almost all migrant workers, called it "jaguar bay," which translated into play B, meaning boards.

They'd all line up and tip the ball against the backboard, letting everyone circle through once or twice until someone usually shouted, "Shoot de ball, Alto Gringo!" They'd buzz around me, laughing, dribbling, speaking in broken Spanish, calling me their token Caucasian. I couldn't have cared less what they called me. I was glad to be playing.

All my life, teachers and coaches would tell Mom I was too fragile for competitive sports, and last year, after Johnny Turbo's elbow took me out of the Valley Leagues, I was desperate for a team, any team. They jokingly called themselves the Wetback Boys, and they were the only ones who would have me.

For close to two hours, I followed Pepper up and down the court. We played Horse, then Pig, and a half-dozen games of one-on-one, and then, without a break, we went back to drills, finally inventing our own, which we called Deuce. It was the popcorn drill with only two people using the full court. Whoever had the ball flashed two fingers and took off down the court, then the other had to follow. The player with the ball laid it up gently against the backboard, and the player who followed tipped it off the board into the basket. It wasn't easy. You had to pace yourself and time it perfectly.

I miss three. Pepper misses four.

"Shit!" she hisses as the fourth one bounces off the rim.

I chase after it.

"Let's take a break." She spits on the blacktop, pawing it with her foot. Neither one of us wants to admit we're tired. She offers me her water bottle, reaches down, and pulls the phone out of her sock to check her messages. Grateful for the water, I take a swig and collapse onto the picnic bench.

"You Facebook?" she asks, thumbs flying, not looking up.

"Nah," I say. I'd changed my last name and erased all online evidence of my former self. Changed my email, too, and now, with no phone, what did it matter?

"You text?" She continues messaging.

I shake my head. "Busted my phone."

She looks up, nods sympathetically, then laughs a little. "Talk about cramping your style, hey?"

The ball Dad gave me is within reach, so I lean over, pick it up, and hug it to my chest. Just to give myself something to do. The leathery smell reminds me of him. Finally, Pepper sets the phone down and lies on top of the picnic table.

We're both slick with sweat.

The wind has shifted—it's blowing off the lake now, and I smell water. Lake Michigan. An ocean smell. Reminds me of surfing, and Dylan, my one and only friend from California. He sold his surfboard before he left for Ecuador. Now he's a foreign exchange student learning Spanish, living in some remote mountain village twenty miles from the nearest Internet café.

"You're good." She closes her eyes. She's breathing heavy.

Still holding the ball, I lie back on the bench and listen to her breathe. I want to say something, but my tongue's in a knot.

"Your Dad's dead, hey?"

Her question feels random, and I sit up again. She keeps talking. "My mom's the one who's gone. Not dead, though she might as well be." She sighs and rolls onto her side, opens her eyes, and then props herself up on one elbow.

Our eyes meet.

"Do you miss him?" she asks me, some expression I can't decipher flashing across her face.

I nod then look away. "Yeah . . . it's kind of complicated."

"I don't miss *her*," Pepper says coldly. Taking the hint that I don't want to talk about it, she lies back down looking up at the sky. "My mom's a liar. I hate liars, don't you?" She turns and stares at me, waiting for an answer.

My throat starts to tighten. "Guess so."

I can't seem to look at her. I'm used to being around guys who brag about their sexual exploits, their bodily functions, or about which girls put out—not personal things. Why does she hate her mom so much, anyway?

She sits up again, wipes at her eyes, and offers me the last swig of water in her bottle. Just as I suck it down, I hear Sunshine call.

"Alyx?"

I hand her the bottle, jump to my feet, and shift the ball under my arm. "Coming!" I holler.

Pepper sits up. "Your mom?" She shades her eyes, studying Mom, who waves from behind the broken porch rail before she goes back inside.

I nod. "Gotta go."

"Radical hair." She squints into the setting sun.

I turn to jog home, but only get a few feet before Pepper leaps off the table behind me and punches the ball out from under my arm.

Startled, I watch her race by, smiling. She snorts out a laugh, scoops up the ball, flashes two fingers, and heads for the far basket. "Deuce!" she shouts, and my body kicks into overdrive as I fly down the court, chasing her.

She's got speed, but my stride is longer. I stay a footfall behind her to make sure I catch enough air when she lays the ball up. When she goes up, I go up. I'm there, perfectly positioned behind her, but instead of laying the ball softly against the board, she pummels it so hard it ricochets off the backboard, and I crash land in the bushes.

Laughing, she takes off running.

"Now we're tied!" she hollers, grabbing her phone off the picnic table, kicking her ball in front of her, and racing toward the pillared house. I stand up, brushing myself off, touching the scrape on my cheek. A prickly branch barely missed my eye.

Collecting Dad's ball, I head home, not sure if I've made an enemy or a friend.

## CHAPTER 8

# Spittin' Image

That night, I lie in Mom's old white-framed twin bed surrounded by the smell of fresh paint, the hum of fish tanks, and the drone of traffic noise. Grizzly painted almost everything in the room lavender — even the wrought iron legs on the fish tank at the end of the bed.

I try not to, but I keep thinking about what Grandpa and Grizzly think.

Really think.

Of me.

*Why does it matter?* I tell myself. *No biggie. They're both bizarre themselves.* Then from the living room, I hear Grandpa say my name.

Instantly alert, I sit up and switch off the aerator on the fish tank. Even more than people staring at me, I hate people talking about me.

"Daddy, it's the middle of the night. Can't this wait 'til morning?"

"Now you listen to me, young lady. California or no California, I've been around eighty-eight years and I never heard such a thing. It's one thing if Alyx's a queer. He needs to know we love him just the same. He don't need to turn himself into a girl! Not that I got a damn thing against girls. You and your mother've been the best gifts of my life. But hell, Liberace was queer, everybody knew it, and we loved him just the same. Grew up next to the Lamperts. Played that damn piano day and night. Once I joined him with my squeezebox at the Legion Center. Boy, did he have an odd taste in jackets though—"

"Daddy! We're not talking about some obscure piano player from the fifties."

"Obscure? That kid became one of the highest paid entertainers of all time. Remember his outfits—looked like they were made of his mother's upholstery."

"I *do* remember. I also remember him having to deny who he was, and you calling him a queer."

"Well, don't you think?"

"Yes, I think."

They grow quiet for a moment, and I can feel my stomach churning. The sour taste of sauerkraut burps up into my mouth. I muffle the sound, quietly get out of bed, and make my way to the door. They start speaking again, only softer now.

"One Christmas he did bring a pretty little thing home with him. She sang, too."

"That was Christina Jorgenson, Daddy, the first transsexual to talk openly about her operation. She was probably born like Alyx, so you see, this is complicated."

"More complicated than pretending he's a girl?"

"*She* isn't pretending anything. *She's* figuring out who *she* is!"

Their voices get loud again. I lean my ear against the crack of light seeping through the door and close my eyes. Must be pretty friggin' weird for Grandpa.

"If Alyx was supposed to be girl then why'd you and Avery make her a boy?"

"We didn't make her anything. Remember what I told you? *Intersex*, they call it." Mom says it soft and slow, so that I have to strain to hear.

"Inner—what? Speak English, girl."

"Shushhh!"

"The kid's got sadness in his eyes, Sunny, way beyond fifteen years. I just don't want to see 'im suffer."

"You think I do?"

"Maybe if Avery'd laid off that dope, the kid wouldn't be dealing with this."

*Touché, Grandpa.*

I wait for this comment to push Mom over the edge. Instead, it gets quiet again. But Grandpa does have a point. Even before he got sick, Dad had an appetite for illegal substances, and I'd certainly wondered the same thing myself.

"Leave Avery out of this." Mom's voice gets fierce. "Millions of kids are born this way, and Dr. Royce believes Alyx deserves this chance, and by God, I do, too. So don't you say or do anything to make *her* feel self-conscious, you hear me? Say what you want about me. But this is my child, and I'm the parent here, not you!"

It gets dead silent again. I shift, put my hand on the doorknob, think about opening it and going out there. But what for? Help Mom defend me, or try to explain to Grandpa something he can't possibly understand? What use would it be? I stay put.

"I hope you're right, Sunny. You know, he's the spittin' image of your mama."

"I know *she is*."

"I meant *she*."

There's a long pause, then footsteps in the hall. Knowing Mom wouldn't want me to hear all this, I stand still, barely breathing, until the footsteps retreat.

"Too bad Clara's not here. She'd know what to say. Least the kid likes basketball. Saw him . . . *her* . . . shooting baskets with the Pitmani girl. Kid loves basketball—least it gives us something in common. Something to talk about, I guess."

"Just be nice, Daddy, okay?"

"Who's not nice?"

"Good night, Daddy." Mom sighs, then I hear her feet scamper up the stairs.

I walk silently back to bed, the wood floor cool under my feet, flip the aerator back on, and crawl into bed. After wiping my wet face on Grandma Clara's quilt, I press my cheek against the smooth glass of the fish tank. I want to be pissed at Grandpa.

I can't be.

I mean, the guy is ancient, can hardly hear, can hardly see, and out of the blue his long-lost daughter returns home after being gone for practically forever, and she brings along his only grandchild, who turns out to be a "she" instead of a "he," and Grizzly moves the poor old guy's bedroom into a musty basement with a bunch of carnivorous fish. Who can blame him?

# CHAPTER 9

# Why Is Water Wet?

What must seem super-strange to Grandpa is old news to me. I remember way back in second grade when I was invited to a pool party. Dylan and I had to change in front of each other. Afterward, he asked Mom why my dick was so tiny.

"The penis doesn't make the man," she'd said and warned him not to tease me or she'd put him in a vice grip.

Dylan helped me figure out how different I was from the other guys.

"Alyx, why don't you have balls?" he'd asked me as we walked home a week later. I just shrugged and answered with one of Dad's witticisms. "Why is water wet?"

Later, Dad explained that Dylan and I were born with the same testicular tissue. Only one of my gonads never fully dropped and the other turned into an ovary.

"I'm deformed?" I had said.

Dad got all intense, grabbed my arm. "Not deformed, Alyx. Just my rare and beautiful boy."

I thought he was going to bust out bawling, but he didn't. Just patted my back, lit a cigarette, and walked off, saying he needed to get some air. That was the year he got sick. And after that, we never really talked much about what made me different, or anything else for that matter.

Till the day he died, I remained his beautiful boy.

# CHAPTER 10

# New Normal

I wake to the smell of Grizzly's gut-rot coffee percolating in the kitchen. He's promised me a ride on the first day of school. Mom warned me before she took off for her new job at the hospital that Grizzly can get snarly in the morning.

Not surprising. The guy has a zillion jobs.

Last night, he covered for an on-call mechanic at the municipal garage. The night we got here, he had to run off and work as a bouncer for a private event at O'Riley's Tap around the corner. Today, he's off to his regular gig at Harley Davidson. Mom claims he gets along with the people who work there so well that they took him off the line and put him in management.

Maybe they're all terrified of him?

I'm just grateful that my room is upstairs, and far, far away from his fish-fetish thing. And I am even more relieved to have my own private bathroom.

Standing in front of the bathroom mirror, I groan.

The humidity's turned my hair into a major Rasta-style mess. No amount of product's going to tame it down, not even Dylan's cheap trick—Vaseline!

I hate the hippie-look.

It's okay on Mom, but the Rasta thing is too grungy for my taste. I had my hair trimmed before we left California— only the ends though because I'm growing it out. At an inch a month, by the end of the year I should be able to pull it back in a ponytail.

The label on the conditioner Mom bought reads: ORGANIC GRACE, GUARANTEED TO TAME YOUR INNER LIONESS.

Worth a try, right?

After I shower, I sift through the pile of perfect first-day-of-school outfits I laid out on the floor last night. Khaki shorts, jean shorts, skirts, sandals, or cross-trainers—which I quickly decide are too old, worn, and beat up. Socks, no socks, a rhinestone studded belt, no belt, a black leather belt Grizzly donated to the cause. Too hard-ass, I decide. Silver earrings. Gold earrings. A heart necklace. Maybe no necklace. Finally, I settle on a simple green T-shirt, a plain silver chain, the yin-yang studs Dylan gave me, khaki shorts, and Mom's Birkenstocks. Let's hope they're not too hippie-looking.

In case we're taking Grizzly's bike, I decide skipping the skirt's a better option.

Check the mirror again.

Not bad.

Semi-normal looking. Then I decide to talk Grizzly into driving the Sunbug Mom left parked out front to save money. She now rides the bus to her new job.

In the living room, Grandpa's out. Slouched down, chin on his chest, his La-Z-Boy tilted back as far as it can go. The sound of his snoring fills the room.

"Grandpa?" I touch his shoulder.

"Someone turn that damn grinder off," he mumbles, waving a wrinkled arm in the air.

"You want help getting to bed?"

"No," he coughs. "Thanks, son, I'm fine." His eyes flutter open, shut again. "Spittin' image. Clara'd know what . . . to do." Instantly he's back to sleep.

"Thinks he's back at the factory makin' sausage. Happens every morning." Grizzly tromps through the living room on his way to the kitchen. "Don't bother with 'im. He won't move 'til noon."

I follow Grizzly to the kitchen table, where Mom's left a note and my lunch.

She opposes school lunches.

"Any organization that counts ketchup as a vegetable," she says, "can't be relied on for sound nutritional advice."

For some reason, she's super paranoid about chemicals getting into my body. Even normal stuff that everyone consumes like coffee or espresso or anything with caffeine, and she's totally militant about corn syrup or fake sugar—or anything resembling sugar.

Seriously.

Even thinking about sugar makes her have to stop whatever she's doing and do deep Pranayama Yoga breathing. That's how wigged-out she gets. And God help anyone who blows secondhand smoke in her general direction.

I sneak a peek in the bag. It contains freshly ground peanut butter on organic whole-grain gluten-free bread, cut carrots, and four fake Fig Newtons made with real honey, which is as close as she ever gets to junk food. I don't mind; most of the time it's passable for food, and it keeps my face from breaking out.

If you wear braces, you can't have a zitty face, too. There's only so much ugliness the world can handle.

Grizzly looks annoyed. He's rummaging through a kitchen cabinet Mom's already begun to organize. After he digs out a super-sized plastic mug, I ask, "Uncle Grizzly, can we take the Sunbug?"

He pours syrupy black coffee into the mug.

"My bike scare ya?" He's dressed in his unofficial uniform, a black T-shirt, leather vest, blue jeans, and some mean-looking ass-stomping boots. Same as yesterday, and the day before, and the day we arrived.

I put the sugar bowl next to him and shake my head. "Helmet might mess my hair."

He grunts.

Last night, Mom braided his hair like hers. Now Rasta braids aren't bad on her, but on Grizzly, they're downright terrifying. I grab some toast and head back to my room. I've changed in and out of the same outfit three times and my bedroom's a disaster area by the time he's ready.

Grizzly shoehorns himself silently into the Sunbug. He's added a couple of his own bumper stickers to the back: PRO-ACCORDION AND I VOTE and MOTORCYCLES HAVE EQUAL RIGHTS.

"Thanks, Uncle Joe."

He smiles. "Scared shitless?"

"Kind of."

He nods at my hair. "Like your '*do*. It took your mom three hours to get mine just right." He primps his.

I'm too nervous to laugh. At first I didn't plan to ask him, but I do anyway, because I just have to know. "Do I look, you know, like a regular . . . girl?"

He rubs his chin, smiles, and starts the car. "Only thing missing is the leather."

I slap a foot up on the dash.

"Birkenstocks don't count. Too California. Not Milwaukee normal."

"Milwaukee normal?" I punch his arm. "The studded belt's way-cool, but I don't want to get a badass rep on my first day."

"Better a badass rep than a badass beating," he says to himself, giggles, and guns the car, leaving a trail of burned rubber in our wake.

It's a whole new definition of normal.

## CHAPTER 11

# Double Winner

After the 7-Eleven disaster, Mom came out fighting for me. I think she was scared, too. She'd talked to every doctor in California who'd ever examined me. She talked to my former shrink in Berkeley and her own internist, as well as mine. She talked to her medical friends at the hospital. She talked to sex-reassignment clinics all over the US and even in Denmark. Finally, she managed to snag an appointment with a famous pediatric endocrinologist, a former colleague of Dad's, Dr. Rene Royce.

Dr. Royce specialized in helping kids like me.

Only, on the phone, he told Mom he rarely worked with teens. Most of his patients were infants and, on occasion, adults. He told her to call back on my eighteenth birthday.

Mom wouldn't take no for an answer, though. She knew a suicidal kid when she saw one. Dad had just died, and she wasn't about to lose me, too.

That whole day is imprinted on my brain—the Sunbug almost stalling out in traffic on the Golden Gate Bridge, me getting whisked into the examining room at Dr. Royce's office. The smell of sage plants lining the windows, and the nurse saying, "Don't worry, Alyx. Dr. Royce is the best in the business," as she hands me a paper gown.

After she leaves, I pull off my clothes and wipe at the willowy armpit hair that I hadn't had the guts to shave off yet. Sweat drips down my sides. I fold everything neatly, setting it on the chair. In the mirror above the sink, I examine my uncertain breasts, touching one nipple lightly. A shiver runs down my spine as I stare at the pubic hair that had popped out around my sorry excuse for a dick.

To this day, I have a hard time looking at the thing.

If only Mom and Dad had just made me a girl in the first place. That's what most parents and medical professionals used to do with babies like me. But, no! My parents had to be politically correct. Wait and see, maybe let me choose. Problem is, they chose first. And secretly, and while he never said it, Dad had wanted a boy. That's why.

Mom probably went along with him because she didn't want anyone cutting into me. I'm her only kid, and when something happens to me, it's like it's happening to her.

Sometimes that's okay, but most of the time she hasn't got a clue what it's like to be me.

After almost twenty minutes, Dr. Royce breezes in wearing purple clogs and a fancy sports watch. Like most doctors I'd met over the years, he doesn't talk much. Dad used to say it was the ones with no personality, "NPs" he called them, who made the finest surgeons. Dr. Royce was a definite "NP."

He flips through the three-inch file from Dr. Matthews and pats the table.

"Let's have a look, Alyx."

I lean back and close my eyes. *Snap, snap, snap* ricochets around the room when he pulls on the rubber gloves.

"I'm just going to palpitate your pelvic region. Try to relax, okay?"

Eyes closed, I nod, hating every minute. His rubbery fingers feel like ice against my thighs.

"How long have you considered yourself a girl, Alyx?"

"Forever."

"Is it tender here?" He pushes down on a lump I've had since birth. When puberty hit, it began to grow.

I open my eyes. "A little."

"Hmmm." He pokes a bit more and then asks, "What's your favorite subject in school?"

"Science."

He grins. "Like Dad, huh?"

I can't help but notice his eyes. The right one's a deep olive green and the left one's the color of the sky. I'd never seen a person like this before. His fingers brush over the lips of my vagina, and I lay there, wishing he'd hurry the hell up.

"Dr. Matthews is right. You're a double winner. Any sign of menstruation?"

"No." Sounding bitter, I prop myself up on my elbows. *Double winner?* It wasn't like I'd won the lottery or anything. I hated to break it to him, but having the dysfunctional organs of both genders didn't make me lucky—didn't make me any kind of winner. Easy for him to say. Dealing with different colored eyes had to be a hell of a lot easier than a dipstick penis.

"Are you almost done?" I ask.

He just keeps probing. "Almost. Are you sexually active?"

*Was he kidding? Who'd want to date me?*

He gently presses around my penis and everything in me wants to bolt off the table. But I stay put. I need this guy way more than he needs me. He pushes on the lump again.

"Ow!" Silently cursing my stupid body, I wonder who wouldn't hate a body that wants to be half of one thing and part of another?

His two-tone eyes zero in on me. "You haven't answered my question."

"No." I looked away, wishing in that moment that I'd just let Prickman and his apes take me out, because wouldn't being dead or even seriously maimed be easier than this?

The truth was I'd never had sex with anybody, not even myself. I'd always avoided touching my screwed-up parts. Covering up my legs with the blanket, his hands travel up my trying-to-be-breasts. He peels off the rubber gloves and throws them in a can, reaches under the paper gown, and squeezes each breast. They aren't much, but still, it hurts. Then part of me leaves my body, and suddenly I'm floating near the ceiling looking down at myself—my freakoid body—waiting for it to be over.

"Did Dr. Matthews talk to you about self-exams?"

Numbed-out, I nod.

"Good." He turns to wash his hands. "Why don't you get dressed, and I'll get your mother, okay?" Without glancing back, he leaves. The minute the door shuts behind him, I scramble off the table and throw my clothes back on.

As I slip on my shoes, I hear Dr. Royce say something to the nurse outside the door and a minute later he's back with Mom.

At first Mom says she doesn't want me to have any surgeries, but when Dr. Royce tells her the not-quite-a-fully-formed gonadal lump is a cancer risk, she does a complete one-eighty and agrees it needs to come out—pronto. But both she and Dr. Royce want me to wait on reconstructive surgery of any kind. Then comes the big blow—Dr. Royce recommends I live as a girl for at least two years before any further surgeries.

In fact, he won't do anything except take out the stupid lump and let me take hormones.

Two friggin' years!

"Alyx, teens with sexual identity and gender issues have an extremely high risk for suicide, so I'll schedule the lumpectomy. We'll put you on a very low dose of estrogen and hopefully that will jumpstart that ovary. Then we'll wait on the rest." He glances over at Mom and then back at me. "It's a lot of change, and I want you to be absolutely certain this is what you want. Understand?"

My stomach seizes up. I look down, study my sandals, feeling both disappointment and gratitude crest over me like gigantic waves. Not now, but someday, I'll be a girl. A real girl. My outsides will match my insides.

We follow him out of the examination room. Mom heads to the front desk to talk about insurance stuff and I head for the bathroom. Gender neutral, of course, but also quiet and private. Locking the door, I smile at my reflection and make a motion like I'm shooting a basket. The only time I felt like I fit in was when I was playing basketball. And plenty of girls play basketball, right? I hadn't even had any surgeries yet, but I stared at my own blue eyes, feeling more like my true self than I ever had. What stared back at me? Mom's fair skin, her high cheekbones and perfect chin, and Dad's long, thin nose, crooked smile, and slightly kinky hair. It wasn't a terrible face.

In that moment, I felt certain that my life could only get better.

I'd be a girl. I'd still play ball. The only thing I'd be giving up would be the daily dish of abuse. I kissed my reflection in the mirror, then wiped off the smeared watermelon lip gloss, knowing Dr. Royce would never have to worry.

I was absolutely certain.

## CHAPTER 12

# Cudahy High

Cudahy High is humongous. In California, Walnut Grove had less than five hundred students in the entire school, which is about the size of the incoming freshman class at Cudahy. Since I never actually graduated from tenth grade because I was absent too much, Mom wanted me to start again as a sophomore.

Another second chance.

She filled out the enrollment paperwork online, then set up a Skype interview with the principal, arranged for me to take some online tests, emailed my scores, and with some fast talk managed to finagle a spot for me in the school's Biology Honors program. Only one other sophomore got in.

Dad would have approved.

"You have a damn-fine mind, kiddo. Use it," he'd say. "Don't do what I did."

I'll be one of a handful of transfers, but I won't be the only new kid on the block.

After Grizzly drops me off, it takes me a little while to locate Room 204, my homeroom. It's Mr. Anderson's science lab, where I have my first-hour class.

It's also perfectly organized in parallel lines. Some DNA mobiles hang from the ceiling. A colored poster above the blackboard reads: ORDER IS BEAUTY. Next to it is a picture of Albert Einstein.

Mr. Anderson's glasses are thicker than Grandpa's, and he's laid out nametags and orientation packets on the desks. It reminds me of grade school in Berkeley, where we lived when Dad was still teaching.

My desk is in the front row. Near the door.

Behind me, a guy named Joel Buck sits down, slaps his nametag on his chest, ignores me, and turns to whisper to the guy behind him. "Peter, my man, I downloaded the app," he motions with a smartphone in his hand.

"Dude, check it out!" The voice sounds familiar. I turn. It's Peter—the same Peter with the camera. He grabs the phone, then sees me. "Alyx? You're in my homeroom!" A grin spreads across his face.

My "hi" is pathetic. I slide the pack off my back and sit down.

A bell sounds in the hall.

"*Girls!*" Mr. Anderson booms from the front podium.

I jump.

"If 204 is your homeroom, please, come in and be seated. If not, please move along before the second bell."

A group of girls gathered in the doorway disperses in a symphony of laughter. The tallest one enters the room breathlessly and takes a seat behind Peter. There's a butterfly tattooed on her right forearm. She's wearing a green top identical to mine, only with blue jeans, flip-flops, and a ton of silver jewelry, rings on every finger—thumbs included.

She sets a flute case down on her desk. A rainbow sticker on the side reads, NEW YORK: GAY STRAIGHT ALLIANCE.

Her confidence and style don't feel "Milwaukee normal" to me, though I'm still trying to figure out what that actually means.

"Roslyn, you guys plan ahead?" Peter winks at her and then at me.

Joel stares at her like someone's whapped him upside the head with a 2x4. I stare, too. Though I don't mean to. She has amazing hair. It's what I'm shooting for. Long. Thick. Wavy. Wheat-colored highlights. Pulled back in a perfect ponytail.

She gives Peter a friendly we-know-each-other grin, then puts a finger to her lips and nods up at Mr. Anderson. He's looking down at his seating chart.

I glance around the room. Only me and my tank top twin have orange orientation folders; everyone else has blue. And no one in the entire classroom's wearing Birkenstocks. Except Mr. Anderson, which wouldn't be so horrifying if his pants weren't at flood height.

*Great! First day and I'm stylin' after a super-nerd science teacher.*

Mr. Anderson stands up and walks to the front of the room. He gives a short welcome speech and with his thin, wiry fingers lists off a litany of rules. Just when I think I've escaped the painful first-day-of-school introductions, he says, "It seems we have two new students." He smiles at me and then at the girl wearing my same shirt. "Perhaps you'll share with us your names and where you're from?"

"I'm Roslyn Rothstein from Long Island, New York," the girl jumps at the chance, answering so fast I fumble for words when Anderson turns to me.

"Uh . . . I'm Alyx—Kowalski." It comes out sounding like Alyx *cold-wall-ski*. I cough and add, "From California." Mom thought with all the changes maybe I should take her surname. She said she didn't want any unexpected publicity that might surface from Dad's past to stick to me, but I didn't want to change my first name. It works for both a boy and a girl, and it's what I'm used to.

I remember wondering who would actually know about Dad's past. He wasn't famous, though his most recent work with DNA and molecular coding impressed certain scientific circles. Still, his greatest notoriety came before I was alive, when he defended the work of the guys in Scotland who cloned the first sheep, Dolly. That same year, he broke all the rules of academia and got involved with one of his graduate students, someone half his age. She got pregnant, so he married her.

That would be none other than Sunshine, my mom. And the baby? Me.

Behind me, Peter whispers something to Joel Buck. They both laugh.

It's not a mean laugh, but I hear the word *hot* several times. I feel my face flush, certain they're talking about Roslyn. I know how guys talk about girls. It's all about conquest and the cool factor, and it's ultra-weird being on the other side.

Anderson doesn't seem to notice anything. After he takes attendance, he sends us out to find our lockers and stash our stuff. I'm standing in the hall, organizing my notebooks and pencils on the top shelf of my locker, when someone taps my shoulder.

"I was wondering who the other newbie was."

I turn around. "Newbie?"

She's drawn little curlicues on her ROSLYN nametag.

"Yeah, that's what they call us around here." She smiles. "Nice shirt."

"You, too—good taste," I try to be friendly back. Remembering what Dylan said before he took off for his remote mountain village in Ecuador: *You gotta make friends, Alyx. Don't be loser loner—it's the only way to survive high school. It'll save your wimp-ass.*

"Pepper said you play basketball. You're trying out for varsity, right? She's totally talked me into it."

"I . . . maybe."

"Well, you better, because on the way to school she bragged you up to Stephanie Wexler."

I stick my lunch bag on top of the pile of books I collected on the way in, grab a pen, and shut the locker door. "Who's Stephanie Wexler?"

"Only the most important girl in the entire senior class," Peter, three lockers away, butts in. "That is, next to my sister, of course." He's sneaking up behind Roslyn, pretending to use her body as a shield. He squints up and down the hallway, wiping imaginary sweat from his forehead. "Man, just watch out for her dad. Even hearing the dude's name freaks me out."

"Wexler! Wexler! Wexler!" Roslyn sings out before explaining, "Stephanie is the principal's daughter."

I like Roslyn already. And I want her hair. She must have ditched her flute case because now she's holding a sketchbook with a purple unicorn on the cover.

"You forgot the important part," Pepper jumps in from somewhere behind us.

She slides up beside her brother.

Peter rolls his eyes. "Pepper's on the prowl for new recruits, fresh meat, Lady Cougars." He smiles directly at me, makes a growling sound, and adds, "Stephanie Wexler is not only the principal's daughter, but she's also the captain of the girls varsity basketball team, the captain of the girls tennis team, and a state-ranked runner. Notice any themes?"

A bell rings right over our heads.

My hands fly up to my ears.

The others don't flinch.

"Five-minute bell." Pepper looks up at the clock. "Listen, Alyx, our best forward moved to Baltimore. I'm the only senior over five-feet-eight, so we're going to need your height. I told Roslyn to get you after school. If it rains, we'll go to the Y. Be ready, okay?"

"Okay," I say, dizzy from how fast she's talking and not sure what I just agreed to.

Pepper grabs Peter and they disappear into the crowd. Roslyn says sheepishly, "I hope it's okay? I told her I would. It's nice to have another newbie in town. This place is sooo different from New York."

I'm opening my locker again to grab the science textbook off the top of the pile. "California, too," I say. Making sure I grab the right book, I shut my locker and stare at the cover.

"You got into Honors Biology?" Roslyn notices the book, which I hadn't paid much attention to until now. I turn it slowly in my hands. It's the last book Dad, Dr. Avery Atlas, had helped edit.

Go figure.

Did Mom know he finished it? Was that why she wanted me to change my name?

Roslyn flicks her finger against the book's cover and laughs. "I tried to get in, but I bombed that online test. Don't look so scared, you'll do fine."

I force my legs in the direction of Anderson's room, making myself walk though I want to run.

How had Dad finished the book with tubes sticking out of every orifice in his body?

Roslyn's still talking. "It's like a basketball cult around here. If you think Pepper's fanatical, you should see her father. The guy sold us our new house, and he's a basketball encyclopedia "

The bell rings again — so unlike the gong sound back in my California high school.

A sudden and surprising pang of homesickness moves through me, more for Dylan than anything, and I wonder what school is like down in Ecuador. His last email said they had dirt floors.

"Gotta go!" Roslyn rushes down the hall with a purple phone in her back pocket just like the one I had until Prickman slam-dunked me onto the pavement.

Standing there, dizzy, light-headed, I wish I could call someone. Mom. Dylan. Even Dad, if he were still alive.

Someone grabs my arm and ushers me into the classroom. "Getting busted by Wexler isn't a good way to start the year." It's Peter again. "Though he must already like you because he's the one who told Pepper to recruit you for basketball."

Wexler, the principal, told Pepper about *me*?

"All the sordid details." He smiles.

*Sordid details?*

I pull away, uncomfortable with being touched. Peter takes his homeroom seat, seeming not to notice, while I try not to act all wigged-out. Usually the only time guys touch me is when they're beating the crap out of me.

I sink into my seat.

# CHAPTER 13

# Pressure

I think about my promise to Dylan. No holing up in the bat cave alone. And though a part of me wants it so badly, I'm not sure playing on a girls basketball team is a good idea, at least not just yet. Plus, there's the problem of the slightly smaller ball, the whole girls locker room scene, and now Peter saying that the principal was talking about me. You'd think in a school with a couple thousand kids, I could just be a number like everyone else.

Then I think about shooting around with Pepper, how great it felt, how I could have played all night if Mom hadn't called me in.

But basketball's a contact sport. I don't care what they say. If I play, I'll be bumping bodies with girls—lots of girls—and even though I'm officially a girl now, too, bumping bodies with anyone terrifies me. I'm not sure I'm even ready for strange guys touching me, either. Even though Peter's good-looking, there's something about him that makes me jumpy.

Still, I can't imagine life without basketball.

I get Pepper.

If I were her, I'd put pressure on me, too.

"Change or die," I whisper to myself. Trying not to short circuit, I set Dad's book down on the desk and close my eyes, thinking about how screwed up everything feels. I'm being recruited to join a team when I'm used to being the faggot picked last.

But no one here needs to know who I used to be, right? Or that Dad's *my* dad. I changed my last name, my email, unfriended everyone on Facebook, became practically anti–social media. I look down at Dad's book. No. One. Needs. To. Know.

This place is supposed to be my do-over. The big cure. A second chance. A real life. Right?

I sneak a quick peek at Peter. Maybe this is a place where I can actually have a few real friends.

"Welcome to Honors Biology," Mr. Anderson's words arc over my head. "Mr. Pitmani, one of our sophomores, has generously offered to be our class monitor. He'll be handing out your assignments."

Peter leans over and smiles. "Anderson loves me as much as Wexler hates me."

Anderson goes on. "Plan to spend at least three hours outside of class for every hour you spend here . . ."

It's not that I'm worried about the work, but as Anderson drones on, I try to remember the Skype interview I'd had prior to coming here. After Dad died, it was like everything just blurred together. What did I tell this Wexler dude?

During the interviewing process, Mom was way more wigged out than me. She isn't the lying type. But she didn't want Cudahy to be a repeat of Walnut Grove. So she did most of the talking. And it wasn't easy, either, for her to cover up the past. I'd skipped school so much.

Now, whenever I think about the past, the guilt about Dad seeps in. It's just there sponging up any extra room in my brain. Poor Dad. I'd made avoiding him a full-time job. Even when he was dying. Instead of going to school, I'd be off shooting baskets all day long behind the 7-Eleven. Then one day I came home with a black eye, compliments of Prickman's pals, and Dad had gone into a coma.

That night Dad died. Quietly. Alone in the next room. He just stopped breathing. Just like that.

I blink my eyes, trying not to think about Dad as Anderson paces back and forth.

In a strange way, I think Mom and me were both relieved, but it was still hard. It seemed like we'd all been waiting forever, and after that Mom set out to save all she had left—me.

So a few lies for survival's sake made sense. And when it came to dealing with Cudahy High, she took the reins. She'd altered my transcripts to reflect some homeschooling she'd given me and sent them on to Wexler, assuring him I was an excellent student and could handle any accelerated science or math they threw at me.

Anderson turns to write something on the board as the memories of Wexler rush into my brain. Of course, it makes perfect sense that he spoke to Stephanie about me. During the interview, all he cared about was my basketball acumen.

"My daughter, Stephanie, is a senior this year," I remember him saying. "She loves the game. Her mother wanted her to take up piano. But like you, Alyx, it's basketball she loves. I should warn you up front, we have a winning tradition here at Cudahy, but the girls basketball program has struggled. This year we're going to change that. You're tall, over six-feet, right?"

Mom nodded. I stared at all the trophies in the case behind Wexler, my face half cut off on the screen.

*Over six-feet, right?*

My height, hopefully, would overshadow what Dylan called my wimp-ass.

Wexler leaned toward his computer camera. "If you're as good as your mother says you are, this year we might actually have a shot at State."

Mom put her hand on my knee apologetically. I didn't hold the basketball talk against her. It's one of the only things she has to brag about.

The bell rings again.

I close Dad's book, get up, and make a dash for the girls bathroom. I've missed most of what Anderson said, but I hear Pepper yell behind me, "See you at lunch!"

Inside the stall, I do some of Mom's breathing exercises.

For some reason my throat is tightening up again. It feels hard to get the air in and out. I feel like I need a shot from Dad's old Darth Vader $O_2$ machine.

Breath is life, right?

# CHAPTER 14
# The Lady Cougars

Not that I really want to, but at lunch I look for Pepper near the milk station. She's not there, which is probably good. I can't help but feeling there's a Prickmanesque quality about her, which worries me. Relieved not to find her, Roslyn sees me—probably looking lost—and flags me down, inviting me to sit with her and a bunch of girls. They're all eating the school lunch, a putrid-looking amalgamation of chipped beef and gray gravy. It smells even worse than it looks—like gas station hot dogs spinning on metal rollers since the turn of the century.

I'm grateful for Mom's sandwich.

Roslyn gets in a few introductions while I manage a couple of bites before my stomach starts churning from the gross smells. Another bell rings. Then we all stampede back to class.

After school, when Roslyn shows up again, I'm outside waiting on the front porch of my house. Rosyln's bummed she couldn't text me, because she was running a little late. Luckily,

Grizzly's at work, Grandpa's napping, and Mom's sleeping off her night shift. No need for awkward introductions or inviting her into the Palace.

Behind Roslyn, standing on the bottom porch step, is an athletic, elegant looking girl with the darkest skin I'd ever seen. She's also drop-dead gorgeous.

"Alyx, MJ's a senior this year, point guard. She plays varsity. Rumor has it she's going to be a surgeon someday." Roslyn puts her arm across the girl's shoulder.

"Speaking of rumors, girl," the girl smiles at me, "you came all the way from sunny California just to join the famous Lady Cougars?"

"Word travels fast," I laugh, making my way down the porch steps.

She laughs, too. "Around here, you'll see that's no lie."

A clap of thunder cracks in the sky and a sudden gust of wind slams the porch swing against the railing behind us.

"Tornado weather?" MJ pulls an ancient flip phone from her pack, checks her messages, and says without looking up, "Come on, let's make a dash."

In California we never got thunderstorms. Tornados either. Only super-thick valley fog.

Under one of the big oak trees, I spot Peter, filming as he runs, his camera pointed at the sky.

"Boy's either missing half his brain or is crazy." MJ shakes her head. "Come on."

We run around the corner, passing O'Riley's Tap, when the heavens open and dump an ocean of freezing rain on us. Screeching with laughter, we fly through the doors of the Y.

To my amazement, Joel Buck from homeroom is standing behind the counter.

"A little wet out there, girls?" he grins. He watches Roslyn dry herself with the edge of her T-shirt. MJ's hair is cropped close and she shakes the wetness onto him.

"Hey!" He puts his arms up. "That's cold!"

"A little ice cold H-two-O!" MJ laughs, turning toward Roslyn and me. "Welcome to Wisss-connn-sin!"

I'm standing there feeling totally naked. My new jog bra is showing through my wet T-shirt, and I wonder without looking if my nipples are showing like Roslyn's are. Though she must wear at least a B or maybe even a C cup, because they are a lot more noticeable than mine. But since I started on the hormones, they've at least grown a bit from their barely budding status.

Joel's staring at me.

I cross my arms across my less-than-ample chest and look down at my shoes. The high tops Mom spent a fortune on are soaked through, and my feet are squishing into the soles.

MJ's trying to explain. "Pepper's dad pays so we can all practice here. Any Cougar athlete can open an account." MJ hands me a pen. I start to shiver, and my hand is all shaky as Joel opens a binder, pulls a form from one of the folders, and pushes it across the counter.

Joel's tall, with huge hazel eyes, a couple of zits on his forehead, and the feeble dusting of a mustache. His face is devoid of meanness. As I check the box marked FEMALE, an invisible noose begins tightening around my neck and that old, familiar panic closes in on my throat.

"Meet us in the gym. You can go through the locker room if you want," Roslyn calls as she trots with MJ down the hall.

"Welcome to the Cudahy cult." Joel takes my form. "If Pepper stays hot, you girls could take State this year. I play, too, but we guys lost three starters. We'll be lucky to make consolation."

Handing me a temporary card, he turns to hook the clipboard back up on a nail behind the desk. Then he whistles softly, winks, and makes a shooting motion with his free hand. He shakes his head wistfully. "Makes me wish I was playing on the girls' team twenty-four-seven—"

The phone rings behind him.

"Thanks," I barely hear myself say, making a dash for the gym.

"YMCA," I hear Joe say behind me, but I feel his eyes on my ass.

## CHAPTER 15

# Pepper's Pissed

Skipping the locker room scene, I head directly for the gym. I'm the first one to arrive. Ditching my bag in the corner, I do a few obligatory stretches, then fumble through the ball bin and grab a women's ball with ample air. It feels small and light in my hands. I can actually palm it, something I can't do with the regulation men's basketball.

A second later, MJ bangs through the locker room door. "Hey, how'd you beat us?"

"I'm fast." I smile at her.

"I'll say." She smiles back as I toss her the ball. She has to take her hands off her hips to catch it. She's tied up her braids in an indigo scarf that matches her T-shirt. She doesn't act like she has supermodel potential, but she does.

As we shoot baskets, she explains that her real name is Matisha Jordan Johnson. She's the youngest of six boys. Everyone thought for sure she'd be number seven. Her brothers had already picked out the name Michael Jordan

Johnson, so when she popped out a girl, her mom kept the initials to keep her brothers happy.

"I know it sounds crazy," she laughs, "I love basketball, but I love school more and someday"—she stops in the middle of a shot—"I'm gonna not only be the first girl born in my family, but the first in my family to go to medical school."

The way she says it leaves no doubt in my mind that she will. And, though neither one of us says anything, it's clear we both recognize there isn't a whole lot of diversity at Cudahy High. Between Roslyn (Jewish), MJ (black), and me (gender queer), we're pretty much it. Of course, they don't know about me, and for now, I plan to keep it that way. It'll be a lot less complicated, and for once in my life I just want to pass as a normal kid.

"Keep shooting like that," MJ grabs a rebound and stands to watch me sink a three-pointer, "we might just take State."

I seem to be making an easy adjustment to the twenty-eight-inch ball. It's probably close to Dad's old ball, which never could hold air. I begin dishing the ball back to MJ whenever I can.

"You meet Stephanie or the others?"

"Only Pepper. She sent Roslyn to pick me up."

MJ stops short. She looks surprised. "Pepper? Patti Pitmani?"

"Yeah."

"Well, you must be something special. Pepper doesn't get along with just anybody. At least not with me."

I want to ask why. But just then Pepper bounces through the door followed by three other girls. One, she introduces as the famous principal's daughter, Stephanie Wexler.

The others are Mary O'Riley and her twin sister, Martha, whose parents own O'Riley's Tap around the corner from the Palace.

They don't mention Grizzly working there. Neither do I.

Stephanie shakes my hand first, firmly. "Hey, Alyx, I'm sorry, it's true, all true. My dad's got this major obsessive-compulsive time compunction problem, but don't worry. You rock if you're into sports. That's really all he cares about."

"Come on, warm up." Pepper grabs Stephanie's arm and pulls her down to the far end of the court.

Martha glances over at my gym bag, which has my name written along the side. I'd blacked out Atlas with a permanent marker and just drew a capitol K after Alyx. She spells it aloud. "*A-l-y-x,* that's awesome. I never saw it spelled that way." She turns to her sister. "I wish I had a name like that. Instead of sounding like some dumb 'Bible babe' who winds up doing all the work for her lazy sister."

Mary hands a smelly sock from her gym bag to Martha, who shoves her sister into Roslyn, who's just run through the door out of breath.

"Wow, so you're the other newbie?" Martha brushes herself off and looks from Roslyn to me. "And you're both sophomores?"

We nod.

"Brilliant!" She laughs looking up at us. "You guys are giants!"

Now Stephanie takes charge, handing out yellow pennies. "Me, Martha, and Alyx against MJ, Mary, and Pepper. Roslyn, you sub in, okay?"

Obviously disappointed, Roslyn retreats to the bleachers.

"I'll sit first," I offer.

Pepper shakes her head.

"Better listen to boss-lady there," MJ whispers as she walks by. "Be careful."

My team has a hard time finding its rhythm at first. Martha tosses up two air balls and then gets shy around the hoop. Stephanie begins to feed me the ball, but Pepper's in my face. Once I discover she can't defend a left pivot, I start to move against her weak side. Twice in a row I set a pick on MJ. Pepper steps up to guard Stephanie, and Stephanie— smooth as ice cream—draws Pepper outside the key and dishes the ball back to me. Already squared up, I hit an easy jumper.

I'm breathing hard but am feeling happy.

MJ barks at Pepper, "Stay with her! I can't stop those."

My team is up one game when MJ sinks a three pointer to even things up. Then Stephanie calls out, "Bubbler break," and dribbles off the court.

"*Bubbler break?*" Roslyn looks back at me. I shrug. We're both lost. MJ puts her arm around Roslyn's shoulder, steering her toward the corner.

Stephanie points to the water fountain and smiles at me. "Hey, Alyx, that's a bubbler."

When it's my turn, Pepper slaps my butt. "Save Lake Michigan for me."

I jump, bumping my head on the porcelain dome.

"Ouch!" Martha shoots Pepper a look. "You okay, Alyx?" she says.

I rub my head.

Pepper laughs. "Sorry."

I can tell she's not.

All of their touching, slapping, and hugging is putting me on edge. When I played basketball with the guys, they did it, too, but this feels different.

Then MJ comes up from behind and drapes her arms around Roslyn and me, squeezing us into a clump. "Once we break you newbies in, this team'll be cruising to State!"

I'm sweating hard now. My hands shoot up to defend myself, like I'm encountering Prickman and his pack. Quickly, I wipe them on my shorts and pretend everything's cool.

Pepper jabs my shoulder. "Alyx, you're pissing me off out there. That's good, really good. That's what we need."

"Oooo, Pepper's pissed, surprise, surprise!" Martha yells. She and Mary slap hands.

Roslyn looks antsy to get in and I need some space from all the physical contact. "I'll sit for a while," I offer, motioning to Roslyn. She grins, blows me kiss, then gives me a high five as she eagerly steps out onto the floor. My heart's pounding. My face is on fire. All this touchy feely stuff is making me a wreck. I smell my own fear and sour sweat like Prickman, only without the essence of ashtray.

Stephanie passes the ball to Roslyn. "Oops, we almost forgot you. Alyx, you stay, I'll go." She jogs off to the side.

I watch Pepper filling her water bottle at the bubbler. "Good for you, Stephanie. There's no 'I' in the word *team*," she calls. "And now, we're gonna kick your ass."

"In your dreams," Martha laughs.

Pepper hacks up a mouthful of spit and sprays it between her teeth in Martha's direction.

Martha groans. "Gross! I swear you act like such a guy sometimes!"

"Well, too bad for you I'm not!" Pepper wiggles her hips, then crosses her arms. "Oh, sorrrrry. Forgot, you go both ways don'tcha—"

Martha's face turns beet-red. Mine feels like molten lava. Mary jumps between them, defending her sister. "Knock it off—"

A ball bonks off the back of Pepper's head. Stephanie means business. "You heard her!"

"Okay, okay." Pepper glances at me, then at Roslyn. She rubs the back of her neck. "Come on, fresh blood—get out there an' show us your stuff."

I jog back onto the court, hoping no one notices how much I'm sweating. I really don't like them hugging me and the musky smell wafting off my body is becoming overpowering— even to me.

Suddenly, MJ busts out into a rendition of Aretha Franklin's "Respect."

When she finishes, she calls to me, "You okay?" Roslyn's with her in mid-court.

I smile, then wave my hand, ignoring the quiver in my belly.

Roslyn slaps the ball between her hands. She calls out the score, "Zero, zero," smiles, slaps the ball a second time, and snaps a pass at me. On autopilot, I catch it, pivot to the left, and sink a turn-around jumper from the top of the key.

Pepper shakes her head. "Shit!"

"Yes!" Roslyn cries.

Stephanie calls from the sidelines, "Newbies rule!"

Points move back and forth until we're tied, 10–10, in our third game.

"Next point takes all!" MJ yells.

Instinctively, I weave through the key while Pepper strains to keep up. Back on the court, moving again, I feel better. I love this game, the feel of leather in my hands, the sound of rubber-soled shoes squeaking on the floor, the breathing bodies gliding over a million layers of shiny floor wax. If Dylan could see me now, he'd be proud.

Pepper plays me close. I've beaten her twice already on an inside shot, so when I move to the top of the key, she tries to shove me with her hip.

She's playing rough, but I hold fast.

MJ fakes a pass to Roslyn and then sends me a bullet. I pivot left, ramming someone as I manage to send off a blind shot. From mid-air I watch, confident as the ball leaves my fingers, knowing it's in the hoop. Then my legs shoot out from under me and I'm crashing down, rolling off Pepper's back. My left hip slams against the hardwood floor. Even harder than the time Prickman made me eat gravel.

"No basket, offensive foul, no basket!" Pepper leaps to her feet jabbing her finger at me. "Charging!" She hops over Roslyn, who's still on the floor. "Moving screen! You have to keep your feet planted."

MJ squares off with her. "You weren't planted! If anything, Alyx should go to the line."

Martha's beside Roslyn. "Roslyn was trying to get out of your way, Pepper. This isn't the guys' Rec League, you know. Can't we have one pickup game without the rescue squad?"

Through her freckles, Pepper's cheeks are flaming red.

Roslyn's crying.

I want to, but I don't. Crying only makes it worse. I learned that lesson a long time ago.

*"At-Ass, you shave your legs! You gay or what?"*

Pepper stomps her foot. "Okay, your game, but you won't get away with this when there's a ref!"

Ponytail pulled tight, Pepper storms out of the gym.

Martha offers Roslyn and me a hand.

Instinctively, I want to bat it away. I don't. Instead, I let her help Roslyn, then get up on my own, wondering if this girls basketball thing is such a good idea after all.

"You okay?" Roslyn sniffles in my direction, brushing herself off.

In the morning, I'll have a bruise, a bad one. Bone deep. Soul deep.

The kind I got in the back lot of the 7-Eleven.

CHAPTER 16

# A Fish for a Friend

At home, Mom sits with Grandpa in the living room. Across one knee, the sailboat pattern of his hooked rug is taking shape. He peers over his glasses when I come in.

"Did you have fun, honey?" Mom says from the sofa, where she's pulling on her white work shoes.

"Uh huh." Stiffly, I make my way down the hall.

"Alyx?" she calls after me. "Are you limping?"

I pretend not to hear, shut my bedroom door, and gently lower myself onto the bed. The goldfish swim up to the side of the tank to stare. A knock sounds at the door. I ignore it.

Mom opens the door a crack. "Honey, I have to take Grandpa to the doctor tomorrow." She pokes her head farther into the room. She's dressed in her nurse's whites. "Can you ask Grizzly to pick you up from school? I'd leave a note, but he doesn't always remember to check the fridge."

"Uh huh."

"There's stir-fry on the stove for your supper." She peers over the fish tank. "You okay?"

"Tired . . . is all." I try to sound steady, calm.

She bites her lip and shuts the door.

The goldfish open and close their mouths in silence. Can fish feel? I imagine them laughing, mouths opening and closing in their silent translucent world. I shift and a shooting pain moves up my legs. Then out of nowhere, Prickman's in my ear: *"Girly-boy, I'm talkin' to you! What? Too much of a wuss to play with the girls? A-l-y-x, that short for Alexandrea? Faggot name if I ever heard one!"*

I curl up next to the tank and pull Grandma Clara's quilt over me, grateful for the hum of the pump that blocks out the voices in my head. Why is this happening? I move thousands of miles away and it's like they're living rent-free in my head.

I tap the tank with my finger. "Blub, blub, blub," I whisper. "What's so funny?"

The spotted fish with a tattered tailfin pushes its mouth into the glass, like it's ready to kiss me.

I smile at it.

"I can't kiss you back until I know what you are? How does it work with you guys?"

I sigh, close my eyes, and let my head drop back onto the pillow. Only the second I shut them, Prickman's there—here—muscles bulging up under his shirtsleeves and his freshly shaved head shining in the afternoon sunlight. The daymares have shifted to nightmares, and it doesn't even feel safe to sleep anymore. Silently, tears force themselves out, and I wipe my face with the quilt.

The tattered fish flicks its tail and darts off behind a plant. It peeks at me from behind the undulating green arms. The other two have intact fins. They hang together.

The spotted fish darts in and out of hiding, occasionally making its way to the side of the tank. I lean my face against the smooth cool surface. Every time I tap, my new friend draws near.

"You got a pronoun?" I whisper, smiling to myself. "Still questioning?"

It feels like she's a girl, but I have no clue, so I decide to call her Q for questioning.

"How about it, Q? I'll be your friend." She flits up near the top of the tank, opening and closing her mouth. She looks sickly compared to the other two.

"I'm Alyx. I'm a *she*." I press my finger up against the tank like we're sealing the deal.

The fish flips twice.

"Hey, nice move. Add a ball and you'll be doing turn-around jumpers in no time."

Flips again.

"And here I thought you were half-dead. Goes to show you can't judge a fish by its fins."

I punch my pillow to puff it up, deciding to skip dinner and let myself sleep. My hip hurts too much to move around anyway.

I'd just drifted off when a dream about Prickman and his bozo-buddies startles me awake. I bolt upright, choking for breath. Their voices bellow in a sick chorus: *"Did you miss us? You're tall, but you're a wimp, aren't you, At-Hole? What're ya doin' at our store, anyway? You gay? You a faggot? Three-points. Yeah, no friends for freaks. Huh, now you're talkin' to fish. What a queer-ass loser!"*

Exhaling forcefully, I try to shake it off, hoping Prickman and his apes won't haunt me all night.

I tap the fish tank. Q fish is there instantly. To derail my brain, I start talking: "Been sleeping in this room for a while and haven't given you guys the time of day. Have I? Who's been feeding you, anyway?"

Q hangs near the top, staring, her gills steadily moving in and out. I decide I'll offer Grizzly to help feed the fish in the morning. The thought of having a fish for a friend makes me feel less lonely.

"Thanks," I whisper, but Q just keeps staring and I can't go back to sleep.

## CHAPTER 17

# Tryouts

In the weeks that follow, I show up for every pickup game. We're outside when the weather is good and at the Y when it's wet and cold. Now that it's November, that's every day. I give Pepper plenty of space, handing her the ball every chance I get. It's confusing, though, because instead of appreciating it, she acts all pissy.

"That girl's like a greased roller coaster," MJ exclaims the day before tryouts. "No tellin' which way she's gonna turn."

Pepper's just stomped off into the Y locker room after MJ knocked her down in the process of stealing a ball. Secretly, I side with MJ, even though Pepper's on my team. To make matters worse, MJ scored and our team lost.

Pepper hates to lose.

"She's got issues," Roslyn mutters.

"You think?" Mary shakes her head.

"Maybe she forgot her meds," Martha sighs and collapses on the floor to rest beside me.

"Someone better give her a double dose." Mary taps her finger to her head. "Something's off."

As usual, Stephanie runs after Pepper.

"Why's she running after that girl's sorry ass?" MJ starts twirling a ball on her finger. "That girl's issues feel like tissues—they're never going to run out and I'm tired of her thinking she's so hot." MJ looks at me, then winks. "We could win State without her. We've got Alyx now."

All the way home, I think about what MJ said. That night, I dream Pepper's dad hired a ref for our pickup games. It's Prickman. He's wearing an official black-and-white striped shirt, only the stripes are going the wrong way and his shaved head is so shiny under the gym lights that it blinds me and the ball bonks into my face.

I wake with a start. It's still dark outside. My room is freezing, and my heart's beating a million miles a minute. I leap out of bed and dash for the shower. Standing under the hot water, forever, calms me. After pulling on a pair of jeans and the green T-shirt I haven't worn since the first day of school, I switch out my silver studs for the yin-yang earrings Dylan gave me.

Grizzly tromps into the kitchen and grunts good morning. I grunt back. He smiles, squinting at Mom's note on the fridge.

"You want me to pick ya up after tryouts?"

Before I can answer, the phone rings, and we both jump. It's turned up impossibly loud so Grandpa will hear it.

"What the hell?" Grizzly grabs it. "Hello?"

He turns toward the window.

"Who?" he demands. "Yeah, she's here." He hands the receiver to me mouthing, "Little early, isn't it?"

"Hey, Alyx, Stephanie's making me call everyone, apologize for getting so intense." It's Pepper. I can hardly believe it. "You're still coming to tryouts, right?"

I sit there breathing into the phone.

"Peter works at the Electric Café. You like espresso?"

I shift the phone to my other ear. Grizzly's hovering near me, listening.

"Maybe sometime we could go there for a latte?"

When I don't answer, she adds, "Tonight, then? Tryouts? You're coming?"

"Yeah."

I hang up, remembering Peter's comment about Pepper's moods and Martha explaining that maybe she'd forgot to take her meds.

Grizzly grumbles, "Pitbull's girl?"

It's annoying when he gets all parental on me, so I shoot him a look. "Who's Pitbull?"

"Trouble, that's who."

"Look," I say, "her name's Pepper. She invited me somewhere. Don't sweat it, Uncle Joe."

Snorting, Grizzly trudges back down the stairs.

By the end of the school day, my hip, which I'd forgotten about, begins throbbing again. Ignoring it, I double-knot my shoelaces for luck. Coach Chance smiles when I run to the bin for a ball.

"Okay, girls, listen up. I'll be running you through drills and pickup games every night this week. No big deal for most of you. On Friday morning, I'll post the rosters for both varsity and junior varsity. If your name's not listed, please don't give up on basketball. Remember, you're always a winner when you do your best."

At the end of the week, almost half of the thirty girls who showed up for tryouts have opted out on their own. Pepper's been on her best behavior—not a single temper tantrum. Coach looks up and smiles at Roslyn and me as we leave the locker room on Thursday night. *A good sign?*

"I won't sleep a wink." Laughing, Roslyn shoves her flute case into her gym bag and waves as she races for the bus. "Until after tomorrow!"

Laughing, too, I throw my fist in the air and call after her, "Newbies rule!"

It's impossible to feel worried or hopeless with Roslyn around.

Pepper, who followed us outside, hops into a shiny silver Mercedes parked by the curb. I've seen the car in front of her humongo house. The license plates read BJ REALTY. The man in the driver seat scowls at Grizzly, who is parked right next to the car.

Grizzly scowls back, then revs his Harley just to be obnoxious.

I slug his arm as I climb on the back of the bike.

Pepper looks away.

Grizzly can't resist revving the engine one more time.

"Uncle Joe, please!" I punch him again.

Before I can ask what his deal is, he lets out the throttle, and all I can do is shut up and hang on.

## CHAPTER 18

# Posted

Next morning I race to the bulletin board outside Coach's office where Roslyn's bouncing from toe to toe. "Yes!" She jerks her arm and spins around. "Yes. Yes. Yes!"

She grabs my hands. "We did it! You and me, baby, we made the big V! Newbies rule!"

Stephanie's name is at the top of the board, followed by the returning players from last season. My eyes dart down past the twins Martha and Mary O'Riley, past Pepper and Matisha Jordan Johnson, past a few other returning juniors: Shana, Jude, and Liz. And there's my name, right above Roslyn's.

Second from last.

My stomach sinks. Someone's scribbled next to my name in red marker CREEPY DYKES NEED NOT APPLY.

Roslyn pats my back. "Ignore it. Some jealous idiot."

The tears just come. I can't help it. Why do I cry so easily these days? I freeze when Roslyn puts her arm around me.

"Alyx, don't take it so personally." She drops her arm as Pepper strolls into the locker room.

I wipe my face and look away.

"Congratulations!" Pepper calls. She breezes up to us. "That dude on the Harley yesterday, he related to you, Alyx?"

"Grizzly, my uncle," I say automatically, my voice sounding like a robot. Blazing behind her head, all I see is the word *dyke*.

She scrunches up her face. "*Grizzly?* That fits."

Roslyn steers me away. "Let's get to class."

I pull back after Pepper turns to her locker. Taking a pen from my backpack, I cross out the offending words, wipe my face one more time, and follow Roslyn out the door.

"That girl is scary," Roslyn whispers as we head down the hall.

I'm only half-listening.

"Hawaii. That's where Joel told me her mom went. It was a huge-ass deal. No one knew where she was at first. People said Mr. Pitmani did her in, and he does sort of look like a Mafia hit man."

I hardly hear her.

*You've just made the big V,* I keep telling myself, yet I can't help but wonder if somehow I've only gone from being a neighborhood faggot to the team dyke.

All through my classes, I try to block out those thoughts. I picture myself hitting turn-around jumpers from the top of the key. I'm moving through the lane like a silent torpedo, sinking outside shots, over and over again, just as the buzzer sounds.

*Basket by number thirty-three, Alyx Kowalskiii!*

It's got a ring to it.

After the final bell, I race to the gym, hoping to change before anyone else gets to practice. As I fly through the locker room door, someone laughs. Coach is sitting behind the thick glass window that separates her office from the locker room. She grins and raps on the glass. "Alyx, don't wear yourself out before practice."

By the time Stephanie and MJ arrive, I'm already dressed.

"Ooooee, oooeee, welcome aboard," MJ coos. "Hell, girl-friend, the way you shoot, I'm glad you're playin' on my team!"

Stephanie gives me a high five. "We're goin' to State this year, so get ready to rock and roll," she sings.

Once everyone's in the gym, Coach has us line up under the basket. All the girls groan, except Roslyn and me, who just look at each other.

"Ah, Coach, it's the first day of practice!" Pepper whines.

"That's right, and I want to see what kind of shape you girls are in. Seniors, you demonstrate our line drill."

The others snicker as MJ, Stephanie, Martha, and Mary join Pepper at the line.

Coach pulls out a stopwatch. "Ready. Set. Go."

MJ takes off like lightning, a smooth-running gazelle leading the herd. Up and back. Up and back. Gracefully touching every line in the gym, she finishes without breaking a sweat.

Stephanie sails in after MJ. The others come in like a cattle stampede, breathing heavily.

"Okay, you girls, ready? Two more sets. Ready? Go!"

"Shit," Pepper whispers behind me.

"That's two more sets for everybody. Compliments of Ms. Pitmani and her mouth. Remember, girls," Coach calls out, "attitude is everything."

Martha and Mary shoot darts at Pepper with their eyes, looking so identical for a split second, I can't tell them apart. I pump my legs until my quads burn. Roslyn finishes beside me and bends over double with a hand on the wall. "I'm gonna puke," she pants.

My legs are trembling when Coach finally lets us sit. Pepper collapses beside me. Our knees accidentally touch and she quickly scoots away, closer to Shana, Jude, and Liz, who clump together in a semicircle, crosslegged.

"Okay, listen up." Coach is grinning. She slaps her hands together, and then her face grows serious as she lays down the rules. No problems with grades, drugs, drinking, or relationship drama. Nothing must become between us and basketball.

We're a team now.

We're sprawled on the gym floor, sweaty, winded, exhausted. Coach paces up and down, twirling her silver whistle.

"This will be your one and only lecture for the season. So listen up!"

She tells us about the girls before us. One decided to cheat on her biology final. Not only did she get caught, but the school suspended her and an F was averaged in with her grades, making her ineligible to play. Then there was the 6-2, 190-pound superstar center who wore super baggy shirts and faked sick to get out of practice so no one would know she was pregnant. When the baby arrived the night before sectional playoffs, her parents yanked her from the team.

We're motionless, a captive audience as Coach covers every potential disaster. She ends with a story from last year, about a girl from West's basketball team who went to a party where some sicko guy slipped something into her drink, then took her away in a van. They found her decomposed body in a ditch the day she was supposed to have graduated from high school.

Roslyn coughs.

When I catch her eye, she whispers, "Intense."

No one else looks fazed. MJ quietly taps out a beat with her hands on the wood floor. Stephanie stares past Coach at the playlist taped on the wall. Pepper's engrossed with her cuticles. They all act like this lecture is business as usual.

I try not to think of a new story: teen-freak-gender-mutant-half-boy basketball player caught with pants down in girl's locker room trying to pass as a girl.

"Questions? Okay, grab a ball."

We spring into action. It feels great to sweat and run drills surrounded by the easy rhythm of bouncing balls, squeaking shoes, and the soft, shrill puffs of Coach's whistle. Basketball distractions are always welcome. They help me feel semi-normal.

During the last five minutes of practice, Coach has us do another series of ball-handling drills with our non-dominant hand. I'm switching the ball to my left hand when the gym door creaks opens. In steps Grizzly.

Laughter stops. Balls stop bouncing. Silence falls over the gym.

I stare. What does he think he's doing? Even Roslyn's staring.

Coach calls, "Can I help you?"

Grizzly grunts something no one can understand and Pepper elbows Shana, then they both burst out laughing.

Coach puts her hand in the air. She hollers, "Girls, back to work!" and heads toward Grizzly.

He points at me. Then shakes hands with Coach.

A minute later, Coach returns, saying we're free to go. She hopes our effort continues all season.

I storm straight outside into the frigid air, the sweat on my shirt stiff in the wind. Whipping open the door of the dented Bug, I yell, "What the hell? My dad's dead and you're not him, so stop checking up on me!"

Grizzly stares straight ahead, flicks the FM rock station off, and starts the car.

"Well?" My hands are on my hips. No one ever talks to him like this. When he doesn't answer, I slam the car door and start walking toward home. He slowly pulls up beside me and rolls down the window.

Gruffly he says, "You'll ruin your shoes, kid."

I pick up my pace. "I don't care!" The hormones bring on tears, making it hard to see.

"I'm driving the bus, all right?"

"What bus?" Why does everyone in my family have to be so friggin' bizarre?

"For your game on Wednesday."

I stop dead. He turns up his leather collar and slows the car down to a crawl. Clouds streak from his nostrils. "One of the guy's from O'Riley's knows your coach. He gave her my name so she called. I was only introducing myself." He sounds almost shy.

I cross my arms. "Since when do you drive a stupid *bus*?"

Grizzly clears his throat and rubs his beard. "Since before you were born. Started when your Grandma Clara got sick.

To help Dad pay the hospital bills. Now it's easy money that'll help your mom. Especially if you trash your new shoes."

Suddenly, I feel like a complete loser. And I'm freezing. I sneeze. Grizzly begins to roll the window up. "I'll wait."

That's all he's going to say. It's enough.

My feet are like two ice blocks. I run back inside, shame sticking to me like Velcro. Most of the girls have already showered and left. Coach's office is dark and the locker room is empty. Only MJ stands completely naked in front of her locker, sprinkling baby powder over every part of herself, sparing nothing.

I cough as I step past her to my own locker.

She giggles, "What took you, girlfriend?"

"Nothin'." I sit down heavily on the bench. My eyes are drawn toward her body, but I force myself to focus on the lockers. Something about seeing people naked makes me feel scared; scared of what I'll see; how different they are from me.

MJ acts so self-assured. Unlike me. Not one friggin' ounce of shame. And, at Cudahy High, in one of the most segregated cities in the country, she has to face being different every day. So, what's my problem? No one knows my secret here. A flash of Prickman dashes through my brain, but weirdly, it's Pepper's voice I hear in my head. *"I hate liars, don't you?"*

"You cold?" MJ stops pulling on her last sock.

I shake my head.

"'Cause you got goose bumps, you know?"

A hot shower sounds good all of a sudden. "Is the water hot?"

"Not worth puttin' your big toe in. It's super hot, but just a trickle. Take you a year to get warm. Except the handicap one on the end. That's why they all fight over it and everyone else goes home to wash." MJ smiles. "They call these showers *ghetto*. Not me. All we've got at home is a tub and my mom says it saves her cash if I wash my beautiful black ass right here." She hops into a pair of skin-tight blue jeans.

Black ass. *At-ass*. Prickman's voice is back. I lean my head against the locker and close my eyes.

"Don't fall asleep," MJ jokes as she leaves. "See you tomorrow, Ms. Sure-shot."

The locker room echoes with emptiness. I kick off my shoes, then strip my damp T-shirt and shorts and sit there for a long time. I know Grizzly's waiting, but I can't seem to move. Everyone is gone and the motion lights go out above me. I'm alone. Safe.

Even when I get up, the lights stay out—only the red exit lights illuminate a path to the showers. I grab my towel and go to check out the handicap stall. It's the only one with a curtain. I yank it back—it's got its own changing area and a full-length mirror.

When I decide it's clean enough, I hang my towel on the hook and make sure the curtain is closed on both sides, in case anyone comes in. Then I strip off my underwear and hit the water, feeling my feet on the cold floor. I stare at my reflection in the mirror, letting the water thaw my back and feet. Gently, I touch the scar on the right side of my pubic bone. It feels tender under the pubic hairs that started showing up last year. Though they aren't much, in the reddish light I admire the outline of my breasts. They only fill an A cup, but so what, right? I like them. They make me feel real, feminine, soft.

Mom bought me a bunch of bras, every color of the rainbow, and a couple with lace. Not sure yet if the super-femi ones are really my style, so I'm sticking mostly with the jog bras. With the help of hormones, my one working ovary has finally kicked into gear, and now I get a light period, which arrives monthly like clockwork. Though my body will never handle a tampon, or a baby, just having a period makes me feel like a real girl.

I stare at the pathetic phallic membrane Dad hoped—with the miracle of reconstructive surgery—would someday become a penis.

I avoid touching it.

It's tucked between two small fat-pads, gonads that refused to grow up. They'll look more labia-like after the next surgery. Then I'll have a clitoris that functions as a urethra, which is a little strange, but better than this baby dick. It constantly reminds me that my first fifteen years masquerading as a boy were a total lie.

I hear snapping towels and voices in the boys locker room on the other side of the wall. I used to hate gym. I would hide when I was in the shower and practically become a professional forger, penning notes from Mom or Dad to get me out of gym class altogether.

The truth is, I've always felt like a girl inside.

"Alyx is too sensitive for a boy," teachers said. "He needs to toughen up."

Someone flushes a toilet in the boys locker room on the other side of the wall. A surge of scalding-hot water spits from the tap as I leap back.

My first surgery was a breeze, but all Dr. Royce did was remove the embedded gonad and that wouldn't have even happened if it weren't for the cancer scare. The second surgery will be more complicated and it won't heal for a while.

I wish it would happen now. I want to look and feel like a real girl, inside and out.

A shriek of laughter erupts on the other side of the wall, then a loud thump. I wait until I hear the boys file into the gym, then I turn the shower off and put my school clothes back on.

Inside the Sunbug, Grizzly's eyes are closed. He's switched the radio to a jazz station.

"Sorry," I say. And I am.

He opens his eyes and shifts into gear.

# CHAPTER 19

# Shame

That night, I lie in bed remembering Dr. Royce's pep talk. "You have *nothing* to be ashamed of," he'd said, standing up and walking to his office window where the Golden Gate Bridge arched into the fog. "It's a big world out there, Alyx. People have all kinds of ideas about what's right and wrong, moral or immoral, natural or an abomination. A person is your enemy only if you give them the power to be so."

He'd stood there in his white lab coat and purple clogs, one blue eye, one green, both fixed on me. "We all have a *right* and an *obligation* to be who we are. In another time or place, Alyx, you would have been revered—honored as a two-spirited one. Native people would have called you a healer, a being who walks in both worlds. They'd have taken you from your parents early on and trained you as a medicine person. You would have been a shaman."

I'd nodded.

"Truth is the mightiest sword you'll ever carry." He'd turned around, his face serious, almost spooky, and he stared right at me. "The eyes are the window of the soul, so whenever anyone tries to make you feel less-than, you look them in the eyes. Refuse to carry any shame. It belongs to them if they're judging you."

I knew in that moment that I'd always feel different than other people. But at least, with his help, if I could do what he said, maybe I'd fit in—somewhere.

## CHAPTER 20

# Wrong Team

With only a week of practice under our belts, we head out for our first game. Grizzly drives the bus. Grandpa insists that he and Mom take a taxi because more than thirty years ago someone broke into Grandpa's car on the North side. Now he doesn't trust *those* people anymore.

Grandpa never *says* mean things about other races, but he talks about crime, drugs, and gangs a lot. Back in the '60s, he says Milwaukee had major race riots. One night at dinner, he talked about when the National Guard was stationed with bayonets right in front of the Polish Palace. Back then, all the black people lived on the North side, until a Catholic priest, a white guy named Father Groppi, marched them over the twenty-seventh viaduct to the South side. That's what started the riots.

"Best thing that ever happened to this city. Brought the bigotry out in the open," Grizzly said, glancing over at me. "At least then people have got to deal with it. Like

Stonewall for the gays. People deserve respect—same rights as everybody else."

"Damn near burnt the city down," Grandpa complained.

I agree with Grizzly, but Mom claims, even now, in spite of the riots, Milwaukee remains one of the most segregated cities in the country. If you ask me, Grandpa's suspicious of anyone or anything that's different. Including me.

As we step into the Bulldog's gymnasium, I look up at the stands and wave. Mom waves back. The Cudahy Cougar cap she crushed down on her Rasta braids looks ridiculous, but lots of other parents are wearing them, too. Beside her, Grandpa's slumped onto a Green Bay Packer stadium chair, hooking away on his rug like he's got a deadline. Two guys are waving from the top row. One of them, dressed in day-glow orange, is holding a sign that reads GO COUGARS! The other's holding a camera with a gigantic zoom lens in front of his face. Joel and Peter.

Peter lowers the camera and waves at me. I look away, feeling completely naked, my cheeks smoldering like hot coals.

Near the timer's table, Grizzly is talking and laughing with a woman who must be MJ's mom. She's an older, more sophisticated MJ. Grizzly's wearing an orange Cougar sweatshirt that makes him look like a giant pumpkin.

"Hey, Alyx, good thing your uncle's our driver." Pepper comes up from behind me and slaps my back. "No one'll try to hijack our bus."

Pepper drapes her arms around Shana and Liz. "Hey, you guys notice how *low* our bus can go. Get it? With Alyx's uncle

94

on board, we have a real low-rider. Don't even have to adjust the tires."

Martha and Mary, who are a bit on the husky side, chime in, "Shut up, Pepper!" Mary then adds, "You're the one with the fat mouth."

"Oh, go chug a beer at the family tap, would ya." Pepper runs ahead of us to the locker room door. "Alyx knows I'm kidding!"

*I do?*

A loud, shrill whistle goes off, and Coach walks briskly past carrying a box of new uniforms. "That's enough, girls. Save your energy for the game."

She calls us over alphabetically and hands us school-issued orange and black uniforms. Since we have to provide our own shoes and socks, we've all decided on white socks with orange stripes. But MJ managed to find a pair of black ones with orange stripes.

"MJ, those are a distraction and not regulation." Coach frowns.

"They're my good-luck socks," MJ argues. "Come on, Coach, they're cool."

"Whose got an extra pair?" Coach calls out. I hold up the three-pack Mom bought and Coach points MJ in my direction.

I toss her a pair. She winks at me, catching them with one hand. "Guess it's my destiny—bein' a distraction," she laughs.

As we head out to the court for warm-ups, I notice MJ's three brothers standing on the top bleacher, all wearing black socks with orange stripes, too. Grizzly, his braids splayed across his shoulders, looks enormous next to MJ's mom where they are seated down in the front row. She's thin and wearing funky glasses that glint in the gym lights. The two of them act like old friends. Peter's now leaning over the side of the bleachers, pointing his camera lens down at Stephanie Wexler. Joel's waving like a maniac, trying to get her attention, then he sees me and mouths my name. Embarrassed, I half-wave.

Joel elbows Peter and Peter's camera immediately swings in my direction.

Quickly I turn away, my throat starting to tighten and my stomach twitching. I sense something subterraneous and dangerous about Peter. Like a burning building, he attracts and repels me at the same time.

The stands are filled. Behind our bench, the faces are almost all white, except for the Johnson family. Behind the Washington bench, the faces are a wide array of browns, dark and light, including the ref who looks like Jackie Lee. He's busy untying a lump of knotted whistles.

Coach calls us under the basket. I force myself to stop worrying about Peter and his stupid camera. Electricity hangs in the air. My stomach's tying itself into knots, making me wish I'd passed on the sausage Grandpa made for supper.

"Okay, girls, here's the starting lineup for tonight's game. MJ, you'll start us out at point guard and Stephanie at second half will make a switch, so you help her out as needed. I want you both to watch what's happening in the key and keep the ball moving. Any chance at an outside shot, take it. Mary and Pepper, I want you in forward positions and remember to fake or set a screen before you pop out."

Martha's face goes gray as Coach puts her hand on my shoulder. "Alyx, you're our center tonight." Coach nods toward the opposing team's center. She's tying her shoes and looks to be about seven feet tall. "Don't let her push you around."

MJ whistles softly. "Toya's one tough-ass mama."

A wave of nausea moves through me when I see Martha's eyes tear up. It's my fault she's lost her starting position, and now, by the look on Pepper's face, she feels demoted, too. Pepper narrows her eyes at me, and I look down at the floor. *Great.*

Roslyn stands behind me and pats my back. "You can do it," she says, as we put our hands together and cheer, "Gooooooo Cougars!" I can't look at Pepper, though. The last place I want to be is on her bad side.

"Bulldogs! Bulldogs! Bulldogs!" The opposing team's audience is stomping and chanting. Their band strikes up some kind of fight song when the buzzer sounds.

"Welcome! Today, Milwaukee's Division I High School Girls Basketball State Champions the Washington Bulldogs host the Cudahy Cougars for the season's kick-off game!"

A roar rises from the crowd.

"Starting at center for the Cudahy Cougars: number thirty-three, six-foot sophomore, Alyx Kowalski."

Coach directs me onto the floor. Above the polite applause, I hear Grizzly bark, "Go, Alyx!"

I don't look up. I can't. I'm too terrified. I run out to the middle of the court, where I stand and stare down at my feet.

"For the Washington Bulldogs, number fifty-two, six-foot-two senior, Toya Woods."

The crowd roars. The band blows a low note on a trumpet. Toya trots up, shakes my hand, then runs back to her side of the floor. Her hand was cool and dry. Mine's hot, sticky with sweat.

"For the Cudahy Cougars, number forty-three, five-eleven senior, Patti Pitmani."

Pepper jogs to the middle. The next Bulldog shakes her hand then she trots over and joins me in line. After Mary and Stephanie join us, the announcer calls out MJ's name. The announcer says it perfectly, "For the Cudahy Cougars, number forty-six, a five-seven senior, Matisha Jordan Johnson."

The Johnson family stands up as one. "Go EmmmJAY!"

The noise in the gymnasium is deafening.

"Play your positions," Coach calls from the sidelines as we set up for the jump ball. Toya stands in the center circle. Planting my foot against the edge of hers, I tilt my body, ready to use my hip if needed.

The ref blows his whistle. He tosses the ball and my body goes up first, but Toya's height works to her advantage. She bumps the ball to a Bulldog guard, who in turn tries to pass it back to her. My hand shoots out, knocking the pass off course. For a second we scramble, then Toya lets out a Herculean grunt before I manage to grab the ball, flinging it to Pepper, who fumbles. A Washington guard lunges for control. Then, the ball pops into the air and the crowd roars as Toya and I leap together, and somehow, I grab the ball. Seizing the opportunity, I turn and race down the court laying up an easy shot—just like I'd done a million times with the wetback boys behind the 7-Eleven.

Laughter erupts in the bleachers. A horn blares. The ref blows his whistle. Coach jumps to her feet, flagging me back to the bench. On the other side of the court, Pepper slaps her forehead and mouths, "O-M-G!"

As I catch my breath, I realize I'm used to playing on half a court with only one basket, and now, I've just gone and scored a basket. For. The. Bulldogs!

*Let me die now!*

Motioning me back to the bench, Coach directs me to the empty chair next to her. "Shake it off, Alyx. Pepper move to center. Martha, go in at forward."

I slump into the chair and bury my face in my hands. "Go, Cougars!" I hear Grizzly shout and all I can think is *Please shut up, Uncle Joe,* because I'm frozen in a solid block of shock and humiliation.

Coach puts her hand on my back. The game has resumed. She glances between me and the action on the floor. I feel warmth from her hand. "Alyx, breathe. You're going back in."

I don't want to. I'd rather crawl in a hole somewhere. Never to be seen again. Tears bump against my eyelids, and it takes every ounce of strength I have to hold them back. Even as a girl, I can't get it right!

"Basket by number twenty-three, Stephanie Wexler. Basket by number fifty-two, Toya Woods. Foul on number forty-three, Patti Pitmani, her third, the Cougars' sixth." The announcer goes on and on.

Pepper's dad jumps to his feet in the second row of bleachers. He's wearing a combat green sweater with BLACKJACK

REALITY stitched under a playing-card logo on the front. Beet-faced, he yells at the ref, "Get some glasses!"

I look at the scoreboard. We're down by one point with three minutes before the half. Pepper's foul has sent Toya to the line. Toya sinks both free throws, putting the Bulldogs up by 3. Pepper looks exhausted and her dad keeps howling from the sidelines. "Patti, plant your feet. You're too far under the boards. Move out. Get your hands in her face!"

I can tell Pepper's trying to ignore his wild gestures, but everyone else can't help but notice him.

Coach presses her hand on my back. "Go in for Pepper."

I start to get up. "Pepper?"

*"Go!"*

Doesn't Coach know what a bad idea this is? Stepping up to the scoring table, I flash my number. "Thirty-three in for forty-three." The ref waves me in. Pepper looks too tired to argue.

"Aw, come on, what are you doin'?" her father yells. "You wanna win or what?"

I look back at Coach, who's watching the scoreboard.

Stephanie catches my eye. Calmly she flashes three fingers in the air, and I immediately forget Pepper and the crowd, moving into position at the top of the key. MJ sets a pick for me, and I fake to the right then pop out. The ball flies from Stephanie to Mary to me. Toya expects me to go right, but I pivot left and knock off an easy shot just inside the key.

"Basket by number thirty-three, Alyx Kowalski."

But soon we're down by 5 when as the last thirty seconds of the first half start to tick off.

As we race down the court on defense, MJ smacks my butt. "Keep shooting girl!"

The next time Stephanie holds up three fingers, she's moving the ball to the left side of the court, playing the post for all it's worth, and Martha's figured this out, so she sets a screen for me as Stephanie loops the ball around her back and comes flying down the center lane. Big, slow Toya steps up to guard Stephanie, leaving me open, and when I catch Stephanie's pass, I use Martha's screen to sink another shot.

With ten seconds left in the half, we're now down by 3.

Stephanie and MJ slap hands as we hustled back on defense. They're both smiling ear to ear. "Block her out, Alyx. No score," MJ says.

Looking winded and pissed-off, Toya stands under the Bulldogs' basket, sweat dripping off her chin. Her point guard, a taupe-colored girl with red ribbons laced into her cornrows, steps outside the three-point line and shoots the ball.

It takes a high bounce off the rim.

Toya and I spring for the rebound, her arm presses against mine, but I make contact with the ball. With rebound in hand, I turn to see MJ take off like lightning, and in one sweet motion, I pump the ball back down the court to her. MJ catches it like a football, stops, plants her feet, and puts up a three-pointer.

It hits as the buzzer sounds.

Wild stomping explodes in the bleachers and the announcer shouts, "Basket good! Tie game. Twenty-seven, twenty-seven at the half!"

Halfway to the locker room, Mom flashes me two thumbs up. I smile, grateful to redeem myself. Stephanie hugs me with her sweaty arms. "Awesome pass, Alyx!"

As the locker room door shuts behind us, Pepper says loudly and slowly, like I'm a total moron, "Remember, we switch sides at half."

"Zip it," Martha tells her.

*Martha, who just lost her starting position because of me, is sticking up for me?*

Mary steps beside her sister. "God, Pepper-puss, it's Alyx's first game. Lay off her already!"

Spitting on the floor, Pepper smears the mucus with the tip of her shoe. Everyone else huddles around a row of benches where Coach has directed the starters to sit. Roslyn stands behind me, loyal as ever, patting my back. She hands me my water bottle. "Small sips."

She shakes her head when I offer to make a space for her. "I've been sitting already." Not a trace of animosity is in her voice and I'm thankful for that.

Coach draws out plays on the chalkboard, says we must use our opponents' weaknesses, warns Pepper to stay out of foul trouble, tells Stephanie and MJ to look for the inside pass, and reminds us all to play team-ball. She smiles at me. "Keep shooting."

I give back a little smile, my braces scraping inside my cheeks.

"New half. New game. Play smart and we'll win this!" Coach continues.

Pepper pokes me with her finger. "*Smart,*" she says into her hand, pretending to cough. I try to slug off the residual shame as we head back out.

By the end of the second half, the Bulldogs have rallied. With three minutes left in the game, they're up by 6 and we're getting tromped in the lane. Even with Martha stepping up to help, I can't keep Toya from scoring without collecting fouls. Soon Pepper and I are both in foul trouble, so Coach begins to rotate Martha in and out of the center position. MJ nails two key three-pointers in a row. Coach calls a time-out. We're down by one point with less than a minute on the clock, both sides of the gym scream their team songs. Flashes of red and white, black and orange shimmer in the stands.

"Fight! Fight! Fight!"

The Bulldogs' fans are completely frenzied, desperate to defend their championship status. Clearly, losing their first game of the new season is not an option.

On the sidelines, Coach grips her clipboard. The black marker squeaks as she outlines a stall play. The girls warming the bench stand so we can sit while Coach hunkers down in front of us.

Roslyn hands me my water bottle, which I make slippery with sweat. I take a grateful swig. Seeing Pepper doesn't have one, Roslyn offers mine, but Pepper pushes it away like it's contaminated.

Coach considers us intensely. To Stephanie and MJ, who look cool as cucumbers, she says, "Our ball, nothing fancy. Keep possession. Wait for the shot. When it's time, feed it to Pepper or Alyx under the board."

They nod and Coach looks from me to Pepper. "Unless we collect a foul, it's coming to one of you."

We head back out onto the floor. I hear Pepper grumble, "If we lose this game by one stupid point, I'll kick your newbie ass."

I pretend not to hear her and set up under the board as instructed, dodging in and out of the paint while MJ and Stephanie weave expertly back and forth, passing the ball. The crowd begins to count down with the clock.

Toya's in my face—we're practically kissing. I search frantically for Pepper. She's double-teamed and MJ, unable to pass the ball into the key, pumps it into the air in the general vicinity of the basket.

*"Four, three, two, one!"* roars the crowd.

The ball bounces off the rim. Both Toya and I leap for the rebound. The ball lands in my hands and automatically I go up for a shot, but the ball slams back into my face, bouncing off the bridge of my nose as the buzzer blares, and Toya crashes down on top of me. The ref's whistle blows above the roar of the crowd, and the announcer calls, "Foul on number fifty-two, Toya Woods."

Cougar fans go berserk—thumping the bleachers, booing, screaming, stomping, and growling.

Stephanie and MJ hoist me up. "You can do it, Alyx!"

*Do what?*

I stand there, dazed, tasting salt, blood, and metal in my mouth. Stephanie and MJ lead me to the free throw line. Leaving. Me. Alone.

I look at the clock. There's no time left. We're still down by one point. Everyone's walking off the floor. All that's left is me and Jackie Lee. Pepper jogs toward the bench, lowering her voice as she runs by, "Okay, Ms. Sure-shot-starter. Pretend it's the Bulldogs' basket. Whatever. Just don't miss."

My stomach's caving in.

The ref hands me the ball. A million pairs of feet pound out fight songs.

The ref nods. "Two shots. Watch the line."

I glance back at the bench. Coach nods. Her arms are crossed.

My legs are trembling so badly, I stamp my feet to stop them. Coach unfolds her arms and holds up one finger. One point's all we need to push the game into overtime. If I make both, we take the game.

I suck in a deep breath, wipe my hands on my shorts.

"Miss, miss, miss," the Bulldogs' fans chant while Cudahy fans call for quiet. Sweat drips in my eye and I quickly wipe it away. I roll the leather ball in my hands, dribble three times, line up, and let go.

*Please, please, please.*

The ball's in, the scoreboard clicks 44–44, and the girls on the bench leap to their feet. Coach reins them in. Retrieving the ball, the ref signals for one more.

The crowd's sudden silence spooks me. My knees wobble as I dribble, and I don't know why, perhaps for reassurance, but I glance at the bench.

Instead of Coach, I see Roslyn furiously snatching my water bottle from Pepper, who's wiping a string of spit from the corner of her mouth. And flying down the bleachers behind them, faster than I ever imagined he could move, is Grizzly, with Pepper's dad hot on his trail. I forget about the stupid shot, the game, everything. All I can think is, *Please, Uncle Joe, don't do anything crazy.* I can't deal with any more humiliation tonight.

I know it's time to end this game.

With one motion, I pop the ball in the air and it whooshes through the net.

A symphony of cheers and groans ensues. People swarm the floor as the announcer cries, "Cudahy Cougars, forty-five. Washington Bulldogs, forty-four."

In a panic, I turn toward the bench, but everyone's in the way.

Usually impossible to miss, Grizzly's nowhere to be seen, and Stephanie and MJ suddenly flank me on either side, slapping hands, patting my butt, my back, my head, anywhere they can reach. I'm hustled into a line to shake hands with the Bulldogs. My legs are Jell-O sticks and my hip aches. Clutching Stephanie's arm, I shuffle along to the locker room with the others. Ahead of us, beaming parents slap our hands as we walk by. People I don't even know are patting me, touching me, congratulating me, but I can't see Mom or Grandpa among them.

"Great game, Alyx!" "Way to go!" "You've got nerves of steel, girl!"

Behind me, the Bulldogs' team has disappeared and the bleachers are quickly emptying out.

"Where's Roslyn? Pepper?" My fingers press into Stephanie's arm.

She peels them away. "Ouch, Alyx! What's with the snakebite? We won!"

"Where's Roslyn?"

MJ is doing a little dance, snapping her fingers, singing, "Ooooeeee, we just rocked the former champs! *Former*— that's the operative word, baby!"

Stephanie and MJ exchange a look when they see me practically crying.

MJ points a thumb back toward the gymnasium and softens her voice, "Something happened back there, but don't worry, they'll work it out." Her hand's resting on my shoulder. "Coach'll handle it. Rozzy put old Pepper-puss in her place."

Martha demonstrates with her empty water bottle. "Yeah, Roslyn sprayed her good."

"Pepper had it coming," Mary nods.

"They're behind the bleachers with Coach," Shana pipes in. "Hope Roslyn doesn't get kicked off the team. Not a bright move to go after our best shooter."

Light-headed, I gulp for air as we make our way to the locker room.

Back on the bus, I don't see Coach or Grizzly anywhere. I collapse into the front seat and close my eyes, afraid that I might puke. When Grizzly finally climbs on board, the chatter hushes. He squeezes into the driver's seat, then without a word, flips the door shut and starts the bus.

"Hey, what about Coach and Pepper?" someone yells from the back.

"Yeah, and Roslyn, too?"

Grizzly acts like he's deaf. He puts the bus in gear.

"Hey, Alyx, does your uncle speak English? Hey, qué pasa? Tell him we're missing about half the team!" Shana yells from the back.

Someone laughs.

Grizzly stands up and turns around. He brushes his braids aside and holds his hand up. He's wearing the black leather fingerless-gloves that hide his badass tattoos.

Everyone shuts up.

"I was asked to take you back. Your coach and the other players have rides." His voice is low. He tries to catch my eye, but I look out the window.

A murmur echoes through the bus as he sits back down. The entire bus shakes, but no one dares to comment on it, and by the time we're back at school, Coach has arrived without Roslyn or Pepper in sight.

*What happened?* I want to ask Coach. I don't even have Roslyn's cell number. But I don't say a thing to anyone, not even Grizzly, and once we're home, I race up the back steps so I won't have to walk past Mom or Grandpa in the living room. Slipping down the hall, I quickly shut my bedroom door.

I hear the buzz of the TV and the *click, click, click* of Grandpa hooking his rug.

"Alyx?" Mom calls out.

A few minutes later, I hear Grizzly clamber up the back steps. He and Mom talk quietly somewhere in the kitchen. Grandpa, who supposedly can't hear anything, says, "Let her be."

*Her!*

It's the first time he's said it without Mom prompting him.

Stiffly, without untying them, I kick off my shoes and peel off my damp socks. The sheets feel cold and clean, unlike my lips, which are crusted with blood. I have no energy to bathe or even brush my teeth. I lie limply in the shadow of the street lamp with Grandma Clara's quilt balled into a pillow to prop my face against the fish tank.

I tap the tank.

"We won."

Q fish swims up to the glass. She opens and closes her mouth like she's nodding.

"I scored a couple of points for the wrong side, but I got them back."

I've decided Q fish is definitely a *she*.

Like me.

The other two goldies sail by, but Q fish stays put. The cool glass against my cheek feels good, and I hear Mom outside my door. She doesn't knock. When her feet finally retreat, I close my eyes, surrendering to the temporary death of sleep, my cheek still pressed against the smooth surface of the fish tank.

# CHAPTER 21

# TWIRP

The next morning at school, Roslyn is standing near my locker, waiting. "God, Alyx, you were like uber-amazing last night. And your uncle's awesomeness incarnate!"

"Are you coming to practice?" I blurt, sounding mad when I'm really just scared.

Roslyn cocks her head and looks at me funny.

"Why wouldn't I?"

I try to not act like a complete mess. "Shana said you might get kicked off the team."

Roslyn laughs. "If they kicked me off, they'd have to kick Pepper off, too. Everyone knows that'll never happen."

I feel so relieved I want to hug her. Instead, I just stand there. The five-minute bell rings and, after the noise subsides, I ask, "So, what happened?"

"I'll tell you on the way to homeroom." She wraps her arm through mine.

I don't mean to, but my body clicks into autopilot and I jerk away. She looks surprised, then hurt, as I awkwardly explain, "I'm still sore from last night."

"Jeeze, don't flip out. I'm not some evil vampire."

"Sorry," I say quickly.

She squeezes my arm gently. "No big deal."

Heading toward homeroom, Roslyn talks fast, "Right before you sank the first free throw, Pepper said, 'This is for good luck,' and spat in your water bottle, then I just lost it. I mean, I got so pissed! I went ballistic. I grabbed the bottle back and sprayed her good. You should have seen her—she tried to scratch my eyeballs out and your uncle came to break it up, and her dad"—she lowers her voice—"that guy's one scary dude. He threatened to get Coach fired if she couldn't control her players. What a joke. I mean, who can control Pepper? She's friggin' outta control. Whether it's ADD or major mental issues, that girl needs help. And then Coach dragged us all behind the bleachers. Pepper started the whole thing and her dad was totally—I'm not exaggerating—over-the-top, out of control. It was such *bullshit!* Your uncle's the only one not afraid of the guy. Finally, Mr. Pitmani grabs Pepper's arm and storms off. Then Coach says, 'Go home,' and that was it. Weird, hey?"

I just stand in a daze. No one, except Mom, has ever defended me like this before.

Roslyn laughs. "*Hey!* You hear that? *Hey!* This is terrifying. I'm getting a Milwaukee accent!"

We're in our seats when the final bell rings. After she sits, Roslyn leans over and whispers, "And, Alyx, I only bite on Sundays."

Bryce Swenson eyes us suspiciously until Roslyn sticks her tongue out at him and then he does the same back to her. I look down at my desk.

MJ warned me about Bryce. Last year, he'd run against her in the school elections as an independent candidate for the Nazi party. "The guy's a loser, Alyx. Walked around with a swastika armband until Wexler caught him putting up racist posters. Sad, huh? Half the school still thinks he's way-cool. But I got elected VP in the end."

At practice, Pepper's quieter than usual.

We don't run any lines. Coach says that last night's game deserves a big reward. Lines fall out of fashion when we're winning, Stephanie assures Roslyn and me. "The more games we win, the fewer lines we run."

That's motivation enough for me.

After practice, in the locker room, I'm not in the mood to talk to anyone. I dress fast while Roslyn keeps yakking. When MJ gets tired of listening to her, she puts her hands over Roslyn's mouth. "Girrrl, give it a rest. You're wearin' out my eardrums."

Roslyn mumbles through MJ's fingers. Soon they're both cracking up.

I envy the way Roslyn collects friends. Even the juniors like Shana—who never used to give Roslyn the time of day—have warmed up to her. That is, when Pepper isn't around. When Pepper's nearby, no one seems to have time for a couple of newbies like Roslyn and me. Even so, I think it bothers Pepper that Roslyn's clearly on my side.

I'm still sitting on the wooden bench inspecting a blister on my foot when MJ snaps her towel near my ear. Instantaneously, Prickman's fist flashes in front of my face and I jump. Everyone laughs.

"Alyx?" says Stephanie as she tussles my hair. "Roslyn's been telling you about TWIRP for ten minutes."

"Sorry." I look up. "Guess I'm tired is all."

"You should be. You ran your beautiful butt off last night," MJ says.

I rub my foot, pretending to concentrate on a blister. MJ stands in front of me buck-naked. Her arms are sinewy, strong, and well-defined from weight workouts. If I pranced around like that someone would need to shoot me and put me out of my misery.

"These showers suck!" Mary steps up next to MJ with a towel around her waist, her breasts mounded like two melons on her rounded belly.

"Yeah, the bubbler's warmer!" Martha adds.

Mary dries her ample breasts with the rough towel. "Well, are you, Alyx?"

"What?" I look up, abandoning the blister, and everyone howls with laughter. Blood rushes to my cheeks.

"Are you guy-shy or what? Are you asking anybody to TWIRP?"

I have no idea what they're talking about so I shrug my shoulders and sit there looking stupid.

Mary grabs a sock from Martha and plops down next to me on the bench. "Roslyn's got her date. What's taking *you* so long?" Mary tries to put the sock on until Martha grabs it back.

"The Y-guy, Joel Buck," Roslyn beams proudly.

"How'd you get him?" MJ puts her hands on her hips indignantly. "He's class president and a senior!"

Mary and Martha stop their tug of war. "Yeah, no fair!"

Playfully, Roslyn yanks Stephanie's ponytail. "You know he's crushed out on *you*, Stephanie. Like every other guy in this school, only he knows you'd never ask him."

MJ raises an eyebrow. She wraps her arm around Stephanie's shoulder. "And who'd you ask, Ms. Stephanie I-can-get-any-man-I-want Wexler?"

"Rick Cleaver."

"Ooos" and "aahs" go off like fireworks, except from Roslyn and me. We have no idea who Rick Cleaver is. Some senior jock, no doubt.

"Cream of the crop." MJ nods. "Not my type, but a fine specimen."

I'm relieved they've forgotten me as they all continue to chatter. The locker room soon clears out except for MJ, the twins, Roslyn, and me.

Roslyn pretends to sneak up behind me. "And you know who Joel's best friends with, Alyx?"

I look up.

"Oh, God, not Peter Pitmani!" Mary says, and they all laugh.

Roslyn slams her locker shut. "What's that supposed to mean?"

Martha and Mary exchange a look. Mary shrugs. "Nothing."

"He's a nice guy!" Roslyn's getting defensive.

"Yeah, I've heard that," MJ grins. "Might want to make sure which team he plays on, if you know what I mean?"

Mary opens her mouth to say something else, but Martha elbows her. They both look at Roslyn, who puts her hands on her hips and turns to me. "He's not gay. That rumor was probably started by some jerk-off jealous jock. And he's uber cute. And Joel says he *wants* Alyx to ask him."

"Hey, all I know is the guy's obsessed, he's always taking pictures of everybody—"

"For the yearbook!" Martha looks at her sister, but Mary keeps going: "I don't care what team he plays on, but any guy with his own darkroom is creepy if you ask me."

"It's his dad's, not his"—Martha shoves Mary gently—"stop spreading rumors."

"I'm not, just sayin' what goes on in the darkroom stays in the darkroom." They start giggling and pushing each other playfully.

I bite down hard, my braces digging into my cheeks.

MJ, who's finished dressing, sashays toward the door. "I gotta go or Mom'll kill me." She nods at Mary and Martha before she disappears.

Whirling around, Roslyn tells Mary and Martha, "Peter's way cooler than Pepper."

Mary doesn't like being reprimanded, even if she agrees. Her voice booms out as she pulls a shirt over her head: "Who cares if the guy's gay, trans, bi, a cross-dresser, whatever, but Alyx deserves to know before you set her up."

Then they start talking over one another. I hear the word *faggot*. My feet want to run. My throat tightens. Grabbing my gym bag and my coat, I race out the door.

## CHAPTER 22

# Who's Gay?

The next day, I realize it's not over. When I arrive at school, Pepper's standing with Roslyn right in front of my locker.

"What's up?" I try not to freak.

"Roslyn says you're gonna ask Peter to the dance."

I cringe.

"Uh, actually . . . I can't go."

Pepper flashes her eyes at Roslyn. Doing a total one-eighty, she snaps, "See, I told you. People think Peter's gay, but she's the real lesbo." And with that, Pepper marches off down the hall.

"God, Pepper," Roslyn calls after her, "way to win friends and influence people!"

I lean my head against the locker. I'm tempted to bang it silly.

"I feel so sorry for Peter," Roslyn sighs.

"What're you thinking?" In drama queen style, I flip my locker door open. "Doesn't Pepper hate me enough? Don't you know when to shut up!"

"It's not like you have a ton of friends." Roslyn's eyes sprout tears. "I thought you and Peter would have a lot in common. You're both braniacs." She hugs her books to her chest as the ten-minute bell goes off.

"Yeah, what else?" I pound my fist on the locker. "Like being the neighborhood faggot?"

Roslyn frowns, her perfect eyebrows arch up together. "What?"

"I mean," I correct myself in a panic, "probably. In any case, I'm sure Peter just wants people to leave him alone, not to be arranging his social life and stuff."

Roslyn walks away without saying a word, and I chase after her.

Finally, she says, "Joel told me Peter wanted you to ask him. Otherwise, I wouldn't have said anything. I thought you'd be happy. Anyway, he's not gay. Joel told me."

Carefully, I reach out and touch her arm with the butterfly tattoo. "Roslyn, Peter doesn't even know me. Why would he want me to ask him?"

She looks at me then says, "Because he met you at the park, and you're in his homeroom, and you're the only other sophomore who got into Anderson's honors class, but mostly, because when he saw you shoot at the wrong basket, you were so cute about it, and he thinks you're pretty." Her eyes beam in on me as a prickly heat starts to consume my body. Sweat starts dripping down the inside of my T-shirt. Roslyn pauses, then continues, "It's not like you have to go alone. Joel and I will double with you guys. Even Pepper wants you to —"

"Why?" I say sarcastically. This just doesn't make any sense.

"I don't know," she hugs her books. "Maybe everyone disses him because he's the opposite of Pepper—funny, sweet, and he hardly ever dates."

"*Is* he gay?"

"God, Alyx! What'd I just tell you?" Exasperated, she rolls her eyes and pulls away.

"I know, maybe he's afraid to come out around here," I sigh and shut my locker gently. "If he is, we could go as friends."

"I thought you *couldn't* go." Roslyn shakes her head. "He had a girlfriend, you know, but their dads hated each other. Now she's hooked up with Bryce Swenson."

"Bryce?"

"Yeah."

After a slight pause, Roslyn asks, "Are you gay, Alyx? Is that why you're worried about Peter? 'Cause it's okay if you are, even if you're bi, whatever. Who cares? My best friend from Long Island's gay, and he's the most amazing guy you'll ever meet. Are you the one afraid to come out?"

"No," I lower my voice. "I mean, I'm just not . . . I've never been on a date." Two of the school's big football stars walk by and my voice fades even more. "Maybe I'm not ready, is all."

"Me either. But what are friends for?" She points her finger at herself. "Like, duh, Alyx. You're my friend, and you could do this for me, you know. I'm new at this school, too, and I'd rather not do the whole first date thing alone either, get it?"

The final bell rings. A bunch of kids scurry past us into Mr. Anderson's room. Bryce Swenson looks up and sneers, "You're late. Tssk, tssk, detention time."

*Speak of the devil.* I can't even look at him.

Why would any girl in her right mind date Bryce Swenson? He stares at Roslyn and licks his lips. She smiles sweetly, then flips him the finger, which just serves to encourage him. I sneak a look in his direction. Roslyn and I are both taller than him. Rosyln by a little; me by a lot. I mouth the words to Roslyn, "Later, okay?"

She nods.

Bryce jabs a nub-nosed pencil into a sharpener on the wall and makes a big show of grinding away in rhythm with his hips as we head for our seats.

As I walk by, he reaches out and grabs my arm. I freeze. "Lover's quarrel?" he grins, yanking me toward him. His hands are strong and his fingers dig into my arm. Every muscle in my body begins to convulse as he puckers his lips and makes a gross sucking noise in my ear. "So, Alyx, is it true what they say about you girl jocks?" His smile widens. "Because you know I like to watch." He releases my arm, but not before squeezing it hard one last time.

A wave of revulsion washes over me as the voices of Prickman and his Neanderthals storm through my brain: *Jesus! Did someone chop it off?*

Not knowing what to do or say, I turn and walk out into the hall, where I break into a run. The halls are empty. I run past rows of lockers, leaping over banged up cases containing trumpets, clarinets, and flutes.

If Bryce only knew what I really looked like without clothes on, he wouldn't want to watch . . .

*Oooo, a real val-e-dick-torian!* An ocean of memories and voices dredged up from my past scream like a mob in my head. It's like every bad encounter I ever had with Prickman starts replaying itself simultaneously in my head. Some strange daymare where Prickman morphs into Bryce and he stands over me, crushing a root beer can in his hand. Sticky foam dribbles down my legs.

*Atlas, what the f—? You shave your legs? You gay, or what?*

I keep running.

Prickman's sour, sweaty, testosterone-fueled ashtray stink fills my nostrils, and the echo of his ape-boys attacks me in a damn chorus. A crescendo of voices chase me down the vacuous hallway as I aim for the exit sign— *Come on. Make 'im fight. We want to* see *'im fight. Watch out. He might like wedgies. Know what I mean? Oh, I'm so scared. What the hell! That ain't a dick! You see that. Jesus, did someone chop it off or what?*

Then I hit something. Hard!

Mr. Wexler grunts as our bodies bounce off each other. He drops a pile of papers when we collide less than ten feet from the front doors. *Damn.*

"I'm . . . sorry." My hands fumble across the floor as I frantically collect his papers and quickly wipe at my eyes.

He looks surprised. "Ms. Kowalski?"

*He remembers my name?* Standing up, I hand him the small stack of papers.

"You're in a hurry."

"Yes, sir."

He looks me up and down, his eyes resting momentarily at my chest while he reshuffles the papers into a neat pile.

"I'm late," I mumble, staring at the floor.

"But aren't you heading in the wrong direction? Isn't your homeroom that way?" He points in the same direction as the little red ducks flying across his tie.

"I . . . uh . . . forgot something."

He blinks then grins at me over his glasses. "You may be forgetful, but the way you bagged those free throws Thursday night impressed us all."

*Bagged?* My eyes meet his.

Reaching down, he collects the remaining papers. His hands are the size of dinner plates. No doubt he was a formidable opponent in his playing days.

"I'm proud of you girls. Coming out of the gates and defeating the State champs is no small feat. Stephanie's hopeful. Looks like she's got a reason to be."

"She's a great point guard, sir."

"She loves the game. She wants to play for the UConn someday. If you girls go to State, it may help her achieve what she's dreamed of since the first day she picked up a ball. Her mother wanted her to stick with piano, but that's not Stephanie. Basketball's in her blood. A true champ, like her old man." He grins wide.

I nod.

The bell rings, he checks his watch, clears his throat, and looks serious again. "Tell Mr. Anderson I detained you. Whatever you forgot can wait. I expect my students to spend their time productively. For you, Ms. Kowalski, that would be on the basketball court, not in detention."

I nod, turn, and escape down the hall. I duck into the girls bathroom and stand stock-still, not breathing. I stare at my reflection in the mirror above the sink.

It's quiet outside the door.

Sucking in a long deep breath, I smooth out my hair. It's getting almost long enough to pull back into a ponytail, though there's still a bit of California surf-frizz at the edges. The hoop earrings Roslyn lent me glitter brightly under the florescent lights.

Tears begin to stream down my face. It's too hard to hold them back.

I stare at myself, hating what I see. I still look like I've always looked, like a sad excuse for a girl—a super-sized, androgynous, super-freak with Grandma Clara's frizz bomb blond hair, Mom's blue eyes, Dad's long, thin nose, and my own limited, special addition, freakfest body.

## CHAPTER 23

# Say Yes

At practice after school, I move through drills as if in a trance. Afterward, Roslyn plops down on the bench beside me. I shift uncomfortably, and I can tell she senses my distance.

"Those lines are killers, aren't they?"

I rummage through my locker, sorting socks.

"Why is your face streaky, Alyx?"

I reach down and untie my shoes.

"Hey, Rossy, you getting excited about TWIRP?" Mary throws her sweaty T-shirt at Roslyn, who jumps up and they begin to talk about the upcoming dance.

Then I hear Roslyn say, "So, you want Peter's number or what?"

Leaning down, she puts her face in mine. "Come on, Alyx. Say yes."

Obviously, she's not giving up on this. "Roslyn," I moan, then close my eyes and pound my head softly against the locker. They all laugh.

"Come on, Alyx, just say yes!" Then they all chant: "Say yes. Say yes. Say yes!"

In my mind's eye, I see Prickman and Bryce standing on either side of Roslyn, sneering, but I hold out my hand anyway. She slaps me five and squishes a small piece of paper into my fist. "Call him, tonight. Okay?"

I roll my eyes. She bumps my shoulder, smiles.

"Don't text him. Oh yeah," she laughs, "you don't have a cell. Even better. Call him, okay—talk to the guy!" She throws her gym bag over her shoulder and heads for the door. "Alyx, you'll see. It's going to be the best night ever! He's totally *hot* for *you*!"

A part of me wants to believe it's true, but something doesn't feel right, and I swallow at the lump rising in my throat.

While Grandpa and Mom are in the living room that evening, I drag the portable black box dial phone into my room and stare at Peter's number that's lying on the bed.

Q fish flutters near the side of the tank.

I tap at the glass and she comes up and kisses it. She's molting, looking even sicklier than usual.

"You're a sorry excuse for a goldfish. But I'm still your friend." Laughing, I flick my finger and she darts back and forth, following it.

I take a breath. Pick up the phone. As if on cue, the fish line up to watch, opening and closing their mouths in unison.

"Here goes," I tell them.

Suddenly the clock chimes nine times in the living room.

It's a convenient excuse. Mom doesn't like me calling anyone after nine at night, unless it's an emergency. Putting the phone down, I decide to wait and ask Peter in the morning at school.

## CHAPTER 24

# Just Do It

The next morning, Grizzly drops me off ten minutes early and I'm waiting near Peter's locker when Roslyn comes skipping up.

"Did you? Did you call him?"

I shake my head.

"Alyx, you promised!"

"I did not."

"You did." She pouts, and I shrug.

"It got late. I didn't want to piss Pepper off."

"Now everything's messed up."

I'm confused, but at that moment Peter comes down the hall, a fancy camera with a huge zoom lens hanging around his neck. He's fussing with the apertures as he walks. That is, until he spots Roslyn and me, then he makes a sharp turn into the boys' bathroom. Is he avoiding me? My brain circuits are in overload.

"I'll ask him when he comes out," I say, not wanting to disappoint her.

"You better, because Joel already told him you're going to." Roslyn struts off toward homeroom.

"Roslyn!" I holler after her. Is Peter feeling pressured, too? Why would he even want to go with me? A part of me just doesn't believe it.

I try to look bored and invisible, scrunching myself down as I lean against the wall. The ten-minute bell rings. A couple of girls from homeroom walk by.

"She's a slut!" one of them squawks.

Probably not about me, but the comment makes me want to run and hide. My heart's racing, the palms of my hands grow sticky with sweat, and something inside of me wants to disappear.

About two minutes before homeroom, Mr. Wexler marches down the hall but Peter still hasn't come out. The principal stops in front of me. "Ms. Kowalski, you're headed for homeroom?"

"Yes," I say and rush off.

When I get to Anderson's classroom, the door is closed and through the slatted window I can see that the lights are out and everyone's watching a movie. Not wanting to think about Peter, or have everyone turn around and stare at me, I head to the library to hang out until the next bell.

All day long, I should be thinking about basketball. Instead, I fume over how Roslyn and Joel conspired behind my back.

And then I keep wondering if Peter's gay. Is that why he hid in the bathroom? But if so, why is he best friends with Joel, who never stops drooling over girls? During practice, neither Roslyn nor Pepper look me in the eye. Even MJ and

Stephanie seem uneasy. Roslyn exits the locker room without telling anyone goodbye. Pepper and the rest follow her out, leaving MJ and me as the lone stragglers.

I slam my locker shut.

"Alyx!" MJ startles and drops a shoe. "What the heck is goin' on?"

"Roslyn's mad. That's what!"

MJ picks up the shoe. "You hit that one dead-on, girl. And how about you?"

"She wants me to ask Peter to TWIRP so we can double with her and Joel. But I haven't yet."

"So, what's the problem? Ask the boy. Is this what Pepper's all hot and bothered 'bout, too?"

"Roslyn says Pepper *wants* me to ask him."

"Hmm, all I know about Pepper is once she realized you could outshoot her, your status changed, big time. From friend to enemy, uh huh, it's happened to all of us in one way or another, and now you stole her limelight, so that daddy of hers is gonna ride her butt to kingdom come."

My heart starts to pound. "She's still a starter. It's not like I replaced her."

"Yeah, well, she's not our hotshot center any more, and she's got competition as lead scorer. From a sophomore!" MJ kicks her locker shut and plops down beside me. "Listen, these Pitmanis, they're used to getting their way. You gonna ask Peter to TWIRP, you'd better just do it or you'll end up regrettin' it all season."

"What's that supposed to mean?" More quietly, I add, "Do you think he actually wants me to?"

MJ stops tying her laces. "Well, you're built kind of sturdy," she reaches over and squeezes my bicep, "in a fragile kind of way. You've got a sweet smile and a few freckles and kind eyes. I can see how a handsome white boy might think that's hot."

She ties up one shoe and switches to the other. "Alyx, you might be a giant, but you're pretty, and that's just what guys like. Peter's pretty, too," she laughs, but it's not a mean laugh. "And I'm not doing him dirt, but I know being pretty, kind of like being black, works against him, especially with the meatheads around here. And let's face it, the guy's a little bizarre, but he's a lot nicer than Pepper. Could be the jocks are just jealous so they spread rumors to keep their women away from him."

*Pretty?* I'm not used to thinking of myself like this.

"Matisha!" A loud voice resounds through the locker room door.

"Mama's gonna skin me alive if I'm late one more time." MJ jumps up. "Do yourself a favor: call that boy tonight, don't drag this thing out, save us all a whole lotta trouble, because it won't help us any at tomorrow's game if Pepper is pissin' and Roslyn is moanin', and you are worrying 'bout your love life. We gotta keep our eyes on the gold—not screw up."

## CHAPTER 25

# Plan B

After supper, I disappear to my room to study for Anderson's midterm.

Apparently, Grizzly, who is not my parent or even a legal guardian, has been tracking my grades on Power School. My blood starts to boil. In a pile next to Dad's laptop, I find Mr. Anderson's science study fact sheet and a few pages about the molecular structure of DNA. Grizzly's printed them out for me.

I pick up the top page. It's an article called "The Exploration of Evolutionary Molecular Codes: From Monkey to Man and Back Again." I look closer.

Dad wrote it!

I check the date. It was published a month after he died.

I flop down on the bed and show it to Q Fish.

"Lung cancer," I say, snapping my finger against the paper. "Never take up smoking."

An image of Dad lying in bed, tubes protruding from his body, flashes through my brain. He blamed himself when I stopped going to school. I blamed him, too. The day I confessed to Mom I'd been skipping school, playing basketball all day, we had a huge fight about Dad. How I thought everything was Dad's fault. How he was the one who wanted a boy. How he couldn't face the fact that he messed up.

It's strange because now I almost feel closer to Dad than when he was alive. I flip his book open on the bed, leaf through it. We hardly ever talked when he was alive. He never touched me, never hugged me, and I can't ever remember him saying he loved me. But I never gave him much of chance. There were days I hated him. I blamed him.

I know he blamed himself, too.

"You know, no one at Cudahy High gives a rip that you're my dad," I say to the book, slamming it shut. "Talk about family secrets. Between you and me, we've got a few, don't we, Dad?" I slip the article in the book, lean over the edge of the bed, and shove the whole mess underneath. Who knows more about the origin of mankind, the molecular structure of DNA, and the reproductive system than me?

"Sorry, Dad, out of sight, out of mind."

"Alyx?" Mom knocks at the door.

"Yeah?"

She opens it and glances around.

"Oh, I thought you were on the phone."

I point to the fish. "My friends field my millions of calls."

"Don't give me that song and dance, Alyx." She sits down on the edge the bed. "You've had that phone in here every night this past week, and the Roslyn girl called three times yesterday, and I just heard you talking to somebody."

"If I had a cell—"

"Don't start." She reaches over and gently touches my chin. "You missed your science class yesterday?"

I pull away. "What, are both you and Uncle Joe tracking me now?"

"We got a call from school. What's going on?"

"Nothing, I was just running a little late. They were watching a movie, and I didn't want to barge in. So I hung out in the library instead."

She glances over at Dad's book. "Is it your father's book? Is that upsetting you? I told you I didn't know he finished it, either."

Shifting out of her reach, I roll my eyes, "Mo-om!"

"Grandpa noticed how quiet you were at dinner."

I refuse to look at her. I hate feeling like an alien from another planet. Tears spring to my eyes.

"Oh, honey, we knew this wouldn't be easy." She puts her hand on my knee. "Maybe we should find someone local, a good therapist, like Dr. Max."

"Don't touch me!" I pull away. "Head-docs are for crazy people. I'm not crazy!"

She looks hurt, which makes me hate myself even more. I glue my eyes to the fish tank. Then the phone rings, so loudly we both jump. Mom grabs it.

"Hello." She sits up straighter. "Sure, I'll check. May I say who's calling?" She pauses before trying to hand me the phone. "Okay, Peter."

*Peter?*

I shake my head in horror, putting up a hand, mouthing no. Mom nods and says cheerfully, "She can't take a call right now." She listens. "Okay, I'll let her know."

With a groan, I bury my face in my hands.

She hangs up and smiles. "He sounds like a nice boy."

I peek through my fingers. "What'd he say?"

"He'll wait near his locker tomorrow if you need to talk with him."

This is getting to be way too much. My mouth drops open as Mom stands up, giving me this annoyingly sympathetic look. "If you need a note, I'll write one, but no more skipping classes, even for the library, okay?"

I nod.

She walks toward the door. "I'm not going to have another repeat of California, so I want to know what's going on with you, you understand, Alyx?"

The top dresser drawer is open. A dirty sock dangles down into the clean ones. Distracted, she picks it up between her fingers. "I'll kill for you, I'll die for you, but I will not let you put dirty socks back in your drawer."

She drops it on the floor. Shaking her head with a smile, she closes the door softly behind her.

As soon as she's gone, I start obsessing about Peter.

What did he really want? Why did he hide in the bathroom today? Why is he always taking pictures all the time, and does he really have his own darkroom like Mary said? Does he really want me to ask him to the dumb dance? Is he gay? Bi? Metro? Like me? Unlikely.

Then I hear Grizzly's heavy steps in the kitchen. He's home early. I get up and switch off the overhead light so he won't find some lame excuse to come in and check on me, or the fish. After a while I hear his voice rise, "I'm telling you, Sis, that whole clan's bad news. Alyx needs to steer clear."

"Oh, that's all rumors and hearsay," Mom dismisses him.

"Wake up, Sunny! Pitmani has a reputation for a reason. Whether the guy's in the mob or the CIA—something's not right over there."

"He's got an entrepreneurial spirit, he sells real estate. Just because he's successful—"

"You play with fire, you're gonna get burned. And that red-head's as unpredictable and dangerous as her old man."

Their voices die down again.

Even though I hate Grizzly acting like the big paren-tal protector, what if he's right about Pepper and her dad? Though it doesn't seem to me that Peter is anything like the two of them. Besides, everyone says he's a good guy. Not like Pepper. At all.

I tap the glass on the fish tank. Q fish swims in place.

"See you in the morning. Don't get in with the wrong crowd while I'm sleeping," I warn.

All night long I toss and turn, dreaming that every time I fire a ball into the air, it lands in the wrong basket. Most bizarre of all, Dad's the referee and he keeps tossing me the ball, then whispering, "Eat spaghetti and try plan B."

CHAPTER 26

# Busted

The next morning, Grizzly agrees to stop at Office Store for
folder tabs. As planned, we arrive at school almost fifteen
minutes late. I've decided to avoid Peter at all costs. I fly into
homeroom, and Mr. Anderson promptly hands me a pink slip,
then sends me back out—to the office.

Wexler raises an eyebrow as if he's been expecting me. He's
standing next to the school secretary's desk.

"Ah, Ms. Kowalski. Do I detect the humble beginnings of
a bad habit?"

I drop my eyes.

He clears his throat. "Please step into my office. The entire
school seems to be suffering from tardy fever this morning."

He points and I see several sets of legs protruding from
chairs beyond the half-open door. Obediently, I traipse into
the crowded room. To my shock and utter horror, Peter, Joel,
and three girls I don't know are sitting there. One of the girls
whispers, "It's the basketball newbie."

"Get along little doggies," Peter sings softly, pretending to strum the expensive-looking camera in his lap like it's a guitar. "Welcome to the Wexler round-up . . ."

The girls erupt in a fit of giggles.

I sit down, the new jeans I put on feel stiffer than cowhide, and the black top I picked out to go with Grizzly's studded belt makes me feel more hard-ass than I want. In another way, it feels like I actually fit in with this crowd, at least for today.

Wexler pokes his head through the door. "I can assure you ladies and gentlemen, your parents will not find this humorous."

We all look at each other and bust out laughing even more after he leaves. In that moment, a part of me likes hanging with the truants and troublemakers.

"Hey," Peter leans toward me.

I pretend not to hear. Joel knocks him with an elbow.

"I'm just seeing if she got my message." Peter slugs Joel back. I ignore them both, pretending to study my nails, grateful I'd brought practically a lifetime supply of pearlescent nail polish with me from California.

"Alyx, I wasn't avoiding you yesterday," Peter tries again. "Wexler was behind you—down the hall. I just didn't want to get busted by him."

Part of me wants to believe him.

Wexler comes back in and shuts the door behind him. On a dry-erase board behind his desk he writes: *8:15 a.m.*

"Can anyone tell me what this means?"

Silence.

"Okay, how about this." Under 8:15 am, he writes *detention*. Then, he writes, *when, where,* and *why*. He sets down the marker. "People, some of you have been in here *every day* this week! I'm tired of repeating myself."

Joel puts up his hand and we all squirm in our seats. Lunchroom smells waft into the room. Chipped beef on toast, again? Gag.

Ignoring Joel, Wexler grabs his marker in disgust. Today he writes after the word *when*. And *room 116* after the word *where*. And *tardy* after the word *why*.

"Mr. Wexler, we have an early practice," Joel's voice quakes. My stomach sinks.

The boys have an early practice because the girls have a home game!

Wexler spins around to face Joel. "You should have thought about that earlier, Mr. Harrison. You may all go back to class."

The three girls stand up and shuffle out the door.

I stand up with Joel and Peter, and my stomach's churning.

Peter watches me. He's stopped singing. He's holding the camera with both hands. I hear him take in a breath.

"Mr. Wexler, sir, Joel and Alyx were late because of *me*." Peter stands up straighter. "It's my fault."

"For the same reason you've been late all week?" Wexler narrows his eyes.

Peter pauses. "No, sir, this time, it's a private matter. Something I need to discuss with you alone."

"As in *now*, Mr. Pitmani?"

If this is an act, it's a good one. The guy's got guts.

Wexler shoos me and then Joel out the door. "Go to class. If Peter tells me anything of relevance, I'll let you know after school when you sign in for your detention." He waves us along.

"Don't worry, Alyx," Joel says, when we reach my home-room. "Peter'll come through for us—he knows who his friends are."

*Friends?*

Joel and I arrive for our detention early, but Wexler lets us off. With a pained smile, he says he knows about Peter's shenanigans and what delayed us.

*What did Peter say?*

On my way to the gym, a trillion scenarios race through my brain and, five minutes into the first half of the game, I'm still obsessing over why Peter took the rap when Coach yanks me to the sidelines.

"Alyx," she says, "focus!"

Peter and Joel are sitting next to Mom and Grandpa in the first row of bleachers. I avoid all eye contact with them. They are all dressed in orange and black. Peter's wearing a shirt with stripes and a hat shaped like a cougar, complete with furry ears. Is it any wonder people think he's weird? But what other people think doesn't even seem to be a blip on his radar screen.

Grizzly's running late. He had a big meeting about the latest Harley gear. Last night he brought home samples, which he let me model, but the studded leather chaps and cap got Grandpa all bent out of shape. Grandpa told me he didn't care if I slept in leather pajamas as long as I held off on the bike business. Said he didn't want to see his only *grandkid* wrapped around a tree.

It didn't miss me that he was being careful with his pronouns.

"Alyx!" Stephanie's in my face.

"Yeah?" I blink, confused.

She grabs my arm and hauls me down the court on defense. "Coach'll bench you if you don't get in the game."

Pepper trots by grinning. "Last week was beginner's luck, Alyx?"

"Blow her," MJ calls. "On offense, they're crowding you on the left. Play the top of the key or go right."

I nod.

A shrill whistle shrieks behind me. West has possession. They throw fast choppy passes, making mincemeat of our defense. I scramble to stay with their center who's shorter than me, but moves like lightning. Twice Pepper calls out a switch under the board and they score on me. Then I miss an easy lob from the baseline, all air, and Coach yanks me out.

"Bye, bye birdie," Pepper hums as Shana prances in from the bench to replace me.

Roslyn pats my back as I slide onto the cold plastic chair.

"I can't believe I missed that," I say, grateful Roslyn's there.

"Everyone has off days," she sighs.

I'm still a little pissed at her for sucking me into the mess with Peter and Pepper. I want to say, *Why would Pepper want me to go to some stupid dance with her bizarro-brother? And why's he hiding in bathrooms, making up excuses, if he wants to go with me anyway?*

But why did he take the rap with Wexler?

A whoop of cheers explode in the bleachers as Pepper steals the ball, hits a basket, and collects a free throw all in one graceful move. Our team moves to the line. We're down by one with twenty-three seconds left in the half. Pepper misses the free throw, but it takes a high bounce and she gets lucky. Grabbing it on the rebound, she pops up and sinks a sweet shot from the top of the key.

West fans groan.

"Um, um, Hot Pepper! Um, um, Hot Pepper!" Cougar fans chant.

Pepper smirks. She's on her home court and it shows.

The air crackles as we head to the locker room at half time.

We huddle on benches as Coach holds up her clipboard, speaking fast, sketching a back-door play. I feel something touch my leg, but when I go to brush it away, nothing's there. Once Coach is done, she heads back out to the court and I stand up, or try to, but instead I fall. Flat. On. My. Face. My knees slam down on the cement floor.

Someone tied my shoelace to the bench leg.

Pepper, Shana, and the gang of juniors behind me burst out laughing.

Martha's furious. "God, you guys, that's not funny!" She and Roslyn reach down to help me.

"We didn't do it," Shana hollers back. "Don't blame us!"

I'm trying not to cry.

Roslyn's angry, too. "Look at her knee!"

"I'm gonna tell Coach," Martha spouts, but Pepper blocks her way.

Mary crosses her arms, joining Martha. "You can't keep us in here for the whole second half."

I shake my leg, rubbing my left knee, which took the brunt of the fall. Roslyn runs to get some ice.

"Yeah, Pepper," says Martha. "Coach'll get suspicious."

Suddenly Pepper turns on Shana. "Sometimes you carry a joke too far."

"Shut up! Whose idea was it anyway?"

"Yeah, but I wouldn't have actually done it!"

"If Pepper told you to jump off a cliff, would you do it?" Mary faces off with Shana as Pepper fades into the background.

Shana's chin begins to tremble. I can see she's crying.

"Shana, you could've really hurt Alyx," says Roslyn, returning with an ice pack and a stack of paper towels. "Is that what you wanted?"

"No!" Shana coughs out a sob and wipes at her nose.

"Come on, we're a team," says Pepper quickly, her tone changing abruptly as she steps closer to the group. "If Alyx is big enough to let this go, we can, too." She smiles at me like we're the best of buddies.

Just in time, MJ pops through the door. "Yooooouuuuu whoooo, game time!"

Pepper lets us by.

Back on the court, Coach examines my knee, irritated, "Alyx, why didn't you tell me you were hurt?"

I open my mouth, but she ushers me back to the bench. The referee summons the players back out onto the floor.

Coach sends Martha in as forward and Pepper as center. She tells Stephanie to switch to a zone defense.

145

Pepper's acting all innocent out on the court.

During the second half, Coach makes only one brief substitution. She sends Roslyn in for Stephanie, so she can review a stall play on the sidelines.

"That was it, my two minutes of fame." Roslyn laughs as she rejoins me minutes later.

"Great pass to MJ," I compliment her. Her cheeks are glowing, and she's all smiles, satisfied that she got even a little game time. Once again, I'm glad she's my friend — even if she sometimes drives me crazy.

Unused to sitting still, my legs bounce up and down, but every time I peel the ice away, my knee looks worse. Red. Puffy.

Shana goes in for MJ. She ignores Stephanie's plays and feeds the ball to Pepper, who keeps banging in the baskets and upping the score until the last three minutes, then we pull ahead when Stephanie sinks a three-pointer inching us into the lead.

Martha calls for a sub after she takes an elbow in the eye. With an eight-point lead and less than two minutes, Coach puts in everyone who's been warming the bench. Except me.

She studies my knee. "That doesn't look good. Let's rest it today."

All the starters return to the bench, without Pepper, who Coach leaves in to cover West's center. Stephanie is ecstatic. She flashes a V for victory into the stands. I look back and see Mr. Wexler wearing one of his famous duck ties, sitting, straight-backed, on the top bleacher. Sure that the game is sewn up, he flashes Stephanie a V back.

When the buzzer sounds, Cudahy fans pour out onto the wood floor yelling and cheering.

"What's with the knee, kid?" Suddenly Grizzly's arm is around my shoulder.

Mom and Grandpa are there, too, and ask to see the damage. I peel away the ice. Mom puts her hands to her mouth. "Oh, Honey."

"It's okay," I lie.

Grizzly scratches his head. "When did you go down? First half?"

Pepper sidles over, Peter and her dad at her side. Peter stares at my knee with a concerned look on his face.

"Hey, good game, Alyx," says Pepper.

I bite my back molars so hard Mom whispers in my ear, "You okay?"

Mr. Pitmani's wearing an orange shirt with the Blackjack Realty playing-card logo. He pats Pepper, then me on the back. I want to barf.

"Yeah, I didn't see Alyx go down," Grizzly growls. He steps toward me to ward them off.

"West is tough, but so are we, right, Alyx?" Pepper covertly defends herself.

Mr. Pitmani beams. "That's my girl."

He smells like stale beer.

Standing with Pepper and her dad makes me want to turn and run as fast as I can in the opposite direction.

Fortunately, Coach comes by and herds us back to the locker room.

When I emerge from the school, Mom's already squeezed in the backseat of the Sunbug. Grandpa leans forward, so I can crawl in next to her.

I lean my head on Mom's shoulder as we drive home. My knee is throbbing and I want to lie in her lap and sleep. Forever. Sometimes I feel like such a baby.

"Do you want to talk about it?" she whispers. She strokes my head, and I get weepy.

Grizzly just drives.

Grandpa's fallen asleep in the passenger seat. He's snoring softly.

Back home, I don't even thank them for coming, just scurry to my bedroom trying not to think about how much I hate Pepper Pitmani.

## CHAPTER 27

# The Cudahy Courier

Grizzly drops me off early the next morning. My knee isn't as red today, but it's tender to the touch, and I limp to my locker not wanting to see or talk to anyone.

When I open my locker, a letter drops out. I pick it up off the floor. My name's written neatly on the outside. I open it. Staring back at me is a note from Pepper:

"Dear Alyx: Hope your knee's okay. I'm doing the next feature piece for the *Cougar Courier*. I want to write an article on what a great basketball player you are. Let's set an interview time at practice. Go Cougars! Pepper."

A postscript is scribbled underneath:

"Peter still doesn't have a date for TWIRP. I'm going with Joel's brother, Clay. Hope to see you there!"

*Is she crazy?* And I decide then and there I'll never give her an interview.

Mr. Anderson hasn't arrived to homeroom yet. A copy of the *Cudahy Courier* sits on every desk. This week's featured athlete is Pepper Pitmani. The cover lists Pepper's accolades. There's also a picture and an article about the dance states that Peter is one of its main organizers. I shove the paper into Dad's book, along with Pepper's note. Why does Peter have to be *her* brother?

From behind her glassed-in office, Coach watches as we file by for practice.

The juniors clump around Pepper, congratulating her on breaking the school scoring record. Shana reads off statistics from the school paper: "Hot Pepper on the Court! Pepper Pitmani's fierce defense on the boards along with an all-time high of twenty-four game points helped Cudahy trounce West in a game that may send the Lady Cougars to State."

Over Shana's shoulder I read the caption beneath the article: "Baby Jocks." There's a picture of one-year-old Pepper playing in a sandbox and next to it a current photo of her all suited up, basketball in hand, smiling in front of her huge house.

"A basketball goddess?" MJ laughs. "Nice spin, Pepper. Write it yourself?"

On the bench, Pepper is sitting, unrolling a pair of socks. "Nope, but I did help write the one on Stephanie last week."

I jog over to the bubbler, remembering how the first time I played with her, Pepper had slammed the ball against the backboard and ran off, laughing.

"Yeah, thanks, Pepper!" Stephanie rolls her eyes. "Next time leave out the interview with my dad. And where'd you get my baby picture, anyway?"

Sucking down the cool water, I listen to Pepper explain how she searched face-prints online and tracked down Stephanie's grade-school yearbook by using her picture.

The juniors giggle in unison.

"No shortage of pictures in that house, I'm sure," MJ whispers behind me.

"Tell Peter he needs a signed release if he's circulating yearbook pics," Stephanie huffs.

"Don't get your undies in a bind. I used our team photo." Pepper laughs and slaps my butt as she and her fan club stroll by. "It's amazing the stuff you can dig up."

The fake lilt in her voice makes me want to puke.


We sit while Coach paces up and down holding her clipboard.

"Okay, girls. First, if you want to take this team to State, last night's game was proof positive that we've got something good going here. We have the depth, the talent, and the ability. That is, if we learn to play like a team." She slaps the clipboard with her hand. "Those joining us for the first time have the good fortune of playing with a seasoned team, a team that realizes every cog in the wheel is critical to our success."

Roslyn nudges my arm.

Coach continues to pace. Her eyes flicker like fireworks. "However, it has come to my attention that certain players caused an altercation in the locker room during half-time last night."

Pepper shoots me a steamy look.

Everyone shifts uneasily, and I stare straight ahead, thinking about how much my life sucks right now.

Coach's voice gets louder. "Shana, could you please spell the word *team* for me."

Shana clears her throat. Her voice wavers. "T-E-A-M."

Coach stops and looks directly at Pepper, "Good. Pepper, you write for the school paper, correct?"

Pepper nods.

"So, as a writer, name one vowel that's never found in the words *my team* or better yet *our team*?"

Pepper studies her fingernails.

Coach slams her clipboard down on a bleacher seat. Roslyn jumps beside me. We're all startled, even Pepper.

"Are you stuck? Seniors, help her out."

In unison the seniors sing, "I."

"Good." Coach resumes her pacing. "Now, how about my juniors? No matter what the final score is, a team player is always a—"

"Winner," they chant.

Coach nods. Next to me, MJ's legs begin to wiggle, while Stephanie lets out a moan and wraps her arms around her knees.

"How about our sophomores?" Coach steps toward us so we have to meet her eyes. "Let's see if you girls have been paying attention."

Roslyn swallows and I run my tongue over my braces, my mouth becoming desert-dry.

Coach's voice raises an octave. "This is basketball-player math, girls. It's simple." A shiver travels down my spine. "On or off the court, the common denominator is what?"

MJ says quietly, "One."

"That's right, 'one team.' Because every player holds what value?"

Roslyn and I look at each other. Everyone else stares at us. A couple of petrified rabbits, we sit side by side, shaking.

Coach laughs, "Come on, I'm not that scary, am I? Come on—"

"*Equal value!*" Almost everyone says at once.

"We are a team—on and off the court. Don't let me see or hear about *anything* that belittles, demeans, or shortchanges any of *our* players. Is that understood?" She picks her clipboard up and points with it toward the door. "Because if anyone has a different definition of team, if any of you want out, *now* is the time to go!"

The only sound in the entire gymnasium is the caged fluorescent light buzzing above us.

"Looks like we have a team, then. For the next three months, we will live, breathe, think, and behave like one. That means we look out for one another. We support one another. We speak out if one of us happens to step out of line. Understood?"

My cheeks grow warm as Coach stares in my direction.

"That's being part of a team, too. If a single player gets hurt, I will be the first to know, got it?"

We all nod, including Pepper, who's shooting me a death-stare.

Coach tucks the clipboard under her arm and claps her hands together. "Good. Line up."

"But we won," Pepper groans.

Coach turns to face her. "Basketball is academic, Ms. Pitmani. As with any subject, we need to go over and over that until we get it right, don't you agree?"

"Narc." Pepper hisses to me under her breath as we line up. I ignore her. Coach keeps us running until my legs feel like they'll fall off. When she finally lets us rest, she assigns us partners—someone to challenge us to play our best.

Roslyn gets stuck with Shana.

Lucky me, I get Pepper. She's as thrilled as I am, and now she's super pissed because she thinks I'm the one who told Coach.

During the drills, I silently avoid eye contact with her.

Our passes are like wild punches, which we slam back and forth at each other. As we weave in and out of the cones, I speed up alternatively whipping the ball at her face or her feet. Making her work. Hard.

Pepper curses under her breath. Coach keeps us running, around and around the gymnasium. The banter of the other girls and the sound of squeaking shoes surround us.

Relentlessly I fire the ball back, wanting to hurt Pepper, inflict pain. Wanting to make her see how it feels to have someone purposely try to hurt and humiliate you.

Then, when Coach's back is turned, she blows a big gob of spit on the ball, and it makes a wet slapping sound as it smacks back into my hands. Now, I'm pissed, too, and I've had just about enough of her, so I purposely fling the ball way over her head, past half-court, and this, finally, tips her over the edge.

Pepper stops. She's winded; she leans over and puts one hand on her knee and with the other she flashes me her middle finger.

I stop, too. She looks up. Her eyes are like two shotgun barrels. Mine are torpedoes, and both of us are fuming with hatred.

"Pepper, get the ball, take five, solo!" Coach is watching, and she's not pleased.

Pepper starts to whine, "Shhheee—"

Coach points to the end of the gym. "Solo! Dribble all five. That will give you something productive to do with your fingers." Then Coach blows her whistle for everyone else to stop.

Panting, soaked in sweat, we all wait for Pepper to dribble five extra laps, then we watch as she collapses to the ground to rest. The other girls are laughing, shaking hands with their partners, but I'm just glad the stupid drills are over. I lean down, rub my sore knee, turn, and head for the bubbler, not bothering to look back.

After practice, Pepper runs up to me in the locker room. Roslyn and MJ glance over but say nothing.

"Alyx, you didn't have to tell Coach." Her eyes are two slivers in her face. "You got my note, right?"

I stare at her, biting down on my lip.

"Here I offer to do something nice. But nooooo, you go and blame me, and I didn't even do it!"

I just look at her.

She throws up her hands "So, you gonna ask Peter to TWIRP, or what?"

Not expecting these words to shoot out of my mouth, I blurt, "What kind of a loser are you? Why would I want to ask *your* brother to some stupid dance?"

Her eyes narrow even more. Stepping back, she pokes her finger at my chest. "First, *you're* the loser. Second, the only stupid thing about Peter is he *wants* you to ask him, which God knows why. And third, Pitmanis *never* lose!"

"You didn't say you were sorry," I spit back, not caring about Peter or the dance or anything else. For once, grateful for the extra testosterone I do have, I step toward her, balling my hands into fists. "You said you *hoped* my knee was okay."

"Same difference!"

"Not!"

She gets right in my face. "What do you want me to do, Alyx? Grovel? And Peter won't either, especially once he realizes who the real liar is." She grabs her gym bag and disappears through the door.

Roslyn and MJ plop down on a bench and begin to quietly peel off damp socks and shoes. It's dead silent in the locker room.

I grab my bag and bolt, splashing home in the rain, sleet, and snow.

CHAPTER 28

# Do or Die

That night, I smuggle Grandpa's phone into my room, throw
Q fish and friends some food, then crawl under Grandma
Clara's quilt and dial Peter's number. Screw Pepper, I'm not
going to let her bully me. Roslyn's right—even Pepper all but
admitted it. Peter likes me, and it's not his fault he got stuck
with her as a sister.

Peter's phone rings twice. "Pitmanis," a gruff male voice
answers.

I gulp. "Is Peter there?"

"Pitmanis," the voice repeats impatiently.

Louder, I say, "Is Peter there?"

"Who's calling?"

"Alyx . . . Atla . . . Kowalski." My voice is wobbling all over
the place.

Silence on the other end, and then I hear something
rumbling around.

"Yeah?"

I almost hang up. "Peter? This is Alyx." *Breathe, Alyx.*

"Who?"

"Alyx." I'm straining to be heard.

"Oh, hey, hi." His voice brightens, then he whispers, "I can barely hear you. It's this damn phone. Listen, long story but can you Skype?"

He waits for me to say more. But my tongue's stuck in my throat. I'll have to use Grizzly's laptop, which probably doesn't even have a mic or a camera.

"Alyx? You still there."

When I still don't speak, he laughs. "I hear you breathing! Okay, how about I hang up and IM you?"

"Okay." I manage to give him my info. After we hang up, I throw myself down on the quilt, groaning into it.

*Why am I such a loser?*

Q fish sticks near the glass, keeping an eye on me. I sit up to stare at the hideous bottom feeder Grizzly recently added to the tank. Its big suckerfish lips are glued to the glass.

"That thing is uglier than you," I say to Q fish, then sit up and point with the phone receiver at the suckerfish. "You're so ugly you don't deserve a name. Go suck all the scum off the bottom of the tank and tell Grizzly to stay the hell out of my room!" I throw the receiver against the door. It cracks into pieces.

*"What in heaven's name is going on in there?"*

Instantly, Mom's footsteps are in the hallway. I grab the receiver pieces and shove them under the quilt just as the door flies open. Mom stands there with Grandpa behind her.

"When's Uncle Joe gonna be home?" I yell at the ceiling.

Mom motions Grandpa back to the living room.

"I need his computer."

"What about your dad's laptop?" Mom glances at my messy desk where Dad's laptop is open, the wallpaper clicking through pictures of every known galaxy in the universe.

"Mo-om. I need to get online." She's clueless about computers.

"Can't you do it from here?"

"*No*! This room has no phone jack, and we supposedly can't afford wireless." I'm stuttering in disgust. "I need a friggin' phone!"

"Don't swear."

"*Friggin'* is not a swear."

"Is this school related?"

"Yeah," I lie, though it sort of is.

"He'll be home around ten."

"Ten!"

Mom's eyes widen. "Fine, call him at work. And what broke? I heard something."

I sigh and lie back on my pillows as she scans the room. "Some privacy, please?"

She puts her hands on her hips, not budging.

I think about telling her the basketball hit something, but she'll just keep standing there with a wounded animal look so I yank back the quilt.

"Really, Alyx, what's gotten into you?" She stares at the little pieces.

"I can fix it."

She takes a step toward me but I put up my hand. "Mom, you always say I need to solve my own problems. I'm fine. Leave, okay?"

Finally, looking hurt and worried, she backs out of the room, reminding me to call Grizzly first before using his computer.

I reassemble the phone and call Grizzly, who gives me permission. As ordered, I don't touch anything in his room except the baby piranhas, which I poke at with a wire net. They know it's not food, so they pretty much ignore it.

I type in Grizzly's password: !-Y-O-B-T-A-F, and smile. His tattoo, backwards.

Then I see Peter's IM under *Pitbullrules—Bingo! Tld Wxler mde U late bball photo shoot 4 yrbk. He wnt 4 it!!!*

I pause. *Thnxs!*

*No prob!*

I pause again. Suck in a deep breath. *U going 2 TWRP?*

An immediate response. *No!*

*U wnt 2 go?*

*Wth U?*

My fingers freeze. Who does he think? He answers before I can.

*Thn yes!!!*

*Grt!*

Breathe, Alyx. *Tlk tom?*

*K.*

*CU*

*CU.*

## CHAPTER 29

# Polka

At dinner the next night, I break the news about the dance to everyone.

"I asked Peter Pitmani to TWIRP."

"Oh, Alyx, that's terrific. I'm off this weekend so we can shop for a dress!" Happily, Mom plops a spoonful of creamed corn on Grandpa's plate.

Grizzly doesn't say a word, just flashes Mom a look. I ignore him. It's not like he's my father, and besides, I hate to break it to him, but people probably think he's just as scary as Mr. Pitmani. Like me, Peter can't help his family.

The next day, Mom and I find the perfect dress made entirely of rich deep-blue velvet with a V-cut back. The matching silk sash actually makes me look like I have hips. I want to wear it home, but Mom talks me out of it. Shoes aren't as easy to find and we have to search almost every store in Milwaukee before we come up with some low-heeled silver pumps. They look classy but, more importantly, I won't tower over Peter anymore than I already do.

When we get home, I model them for Grizzly and Grandpa, who both act like I'm drop-dead gorgeous, which I appreciate. I do the whole bit, makeup and everything, then while Grandpa keeps telling Mom, "Alyx is the spittin' image of my Clara, spittin' image," Grizzly shows me a few dance steps.

He pushes back the furniture as Mom and Grandpa watch from the side. I'm surprised. Grizzly can move. Mom watches for a while then suggests he change his name to John Travolta.

"You mean Revolta." Grizzly makes a gag motion with his finger.

Despite his joking, Grizzly's a good dance teacher. He shows me how to waltz, to two-step, and to swing. I, on the other hand, suck. Mom says, "Just have fun."

Then Grandpa insists on showing me how to polka. He says, "Mark my words, Alyx. I may be an old goat, but Milwaukee's Milwaukee and in Milwaukee, people polka."

He takes my hands and we're off, with me hopping from foot to foot, terrified he's going to keel over, but soon he has to sit and makes Mom take over.

## CHAPTER 30

# Secrets

At exactly seven o'clock, on the night of the dance, Peter arrives in a huge stretch limo. He climbs out with Joel and Roslyn. Mom and I step outside to greet them. Roslyn runs up the steps and, giving me a hug, throws open her wool shawl. Her dress has a beautiful burgundy lace bodice with a sweeping chenille skirt—gorgeous, like her.

She tugs at Mom's wool coat, which I am borrowing. No way am I wearing a ski jacket over a formal dress.

"Let me see what you're wearing, silly."

Obediently, I undo the buttons, hand the coat to Mom, then twirl around, showing off my dress.

Joel whistles.

Goosebumps jump all over my arms, but I don't care. I've been getting ready for exactly five hours and for once, I actually feel pretty!

"Alyx, you look great." Roslyn throws back her head and laughs. She smells of overly sweet perfume and cheap wine.

She squeezes my arm. It's freezing out, and I'm shivering as I pull my coat back on.

Peter steps up and shyly hands me a single, white long-stemmed rose. The biggest rose I've ever seen.

Mom exclaims how beautiful it is and how handsome he and Joel look in their black suits. She shelters the rose from the wind with one hand.

Peter whispers, "I had them take off the thorns so you can bring it along."

I croak out a thank-you.

Mom asks to take some pictures outside. I've forbidden her to invite anyone inside. "It's just a dance," I'd told her. I wasn't ready for Polish Palace tours or Grizzly being snarky to Peter.

Between flashes, I see Grizzly and Grandpa peeking down from behind the blinds in the upstairs window. Mom's got one of those pathetic disposable cameras, so Peter whips a brand new phone out of his pocket and shows Mom how to take our picture with it.

"It takes videos, too!" Peter says when she acts all impressed. I smile with my mouth shut so my braces don't show.

Behind Mom, Grizzly waves from the window, but I'm too distracted to wave back.

After the pictures, Peter helps me with my coat. He looks so elegant and I suddenly feel gawky and clumsy. Mom's eyes open wide when he says we have reservations at Georgiano's. It's one of the most expensive restaurants in Milwaukee. I reach in and finger the hundred-dollar bill she's tucked in my coat pocket. How expensive can pizza or pasta be?

Mom waves.

I wave, then bunch up the skirt of my dress and climb into the limo.

"Can you believe this car? Peter's dad got it for us!" Roslyn giggles. Her eyes are glassy.

"Dad's buddy owns a funeral home," Peter jokes. "Don't worry, I checked the back for bodies."

Joel and Roslyn burst into gales of laughter.

*Breathe*, I have to remind myself, because my body is stone-cold like a cadaver.

"I hope it's okay, Alyx," Peter says suddenly. "Pepper and Clay are setting up for a party at our house later. We'll come back here after the dance, then I'll walk you home."

I must look terrified because Roslyn jumps in. Her cheeks are flushed. She's been sipping from a flask Joel brought along. "Don't worrrrry, Pepper's been great since Alyx ashhhked you to the dance."

She's slurring? Has she lost her mind?

Joel offers me a sip, but I shake my head. Peter takes a huge swig and coughs. "What is this stuff, grain alcohol?"

"Close," Joel laughs.

"Whew!" Peter laughs, too.

"Rules are made to be broken. Right, Alyx?" Joel nudges my foot.

All I can think about is Coach and getting caught, or worse yet, getting kicked off the team.

"Wicked," Roslyn giggles, leaning her head against Joel's shoulder and closing her eyes.

Compared to Joel and Roslyn, who act like they're velcroed at the hip, Peter barely lets his leg lean against mine. He checks his phone, slips it back in his pocket, then reaches over and touches my hand. My cheeks ignite. His warm fingers press gently into mine.

*Breathe*, I remind myself again.

"You have big hands for a girl." My heart wants to leap out of my mouth. "Can you palm a basketball?" he asks casually.

"Shhhe's the only girl who caaan." Roslyn's eyes are closed.

My fingers stretch out a good quarter-inch longer than his.

"A nine-inch ball," I smile, and then quickly look away as the houses fly by beyond the tinted window. *OMG, Alyx, a nine-inch ball? Did you really just say that?*

Grinning, Peter jostles me gently. "Never noticed your hands before. Guess I've been too busy watching you." Our eyes meet. The light reflecting off his perfect teeth momentarily blinds me, blood floods my heart, and unconsciously I run my tongue over my lame-o braces. He squeezes my fingers.

I squeeze back, feeling like I might faint.

At Georgiano's we have our own private waiter, a friend of Peter's dad. Afterward, Roslyn and I pool our money to pay the check. Peter tells the waiter to apply his family discount. Without a tip, my share comes out to exactly fifty dollars. When Peter hands me the change, he leans close. "Thanks, Alyx. Thanks for asking me." His breath is warm and boozy.

Roslyn gushes on the walk back to the limo, "Was that spumoni ice cream good or what?"

At school, kids crowd around the limousine, so Peter has to stay behind a few minutes and give tours. I follow Joel and Roslyn into the gym. Orange and black streamers hang everywhere. Above the basketball hoop, two cartoon Cougars in formal attire—one male, one female—dance on the wall. School colors spell out TWIRP. The whole thing looks like Halloween, minus the witches.

A live band is warming up. Peter finds me standing near a row of chairs. "How about these decorations?"

I nod, then smile, trying to cover my braces with my lips.

He cocks his head to the side. "You don't talk much, do you?"

"They're great," I offer.

He points proudly to the web of streamers hanging from the ceiling. The band begins playing in earnest and a few couples step out onto the floor. "Joel and I helped Wexler get those up with a ladder."

"Wexler?" I can't imagine him on a ladder. Or Peter helping him.

"Wanna dance?" Peter grabs my hand and pulls me into the middle of the floor.

We dance without talking or touching. I do my best not to look too dorky, keeping my back to the idle watchers along the gym wall. Fortunately, it's pretty dark with the dimmed lights. By the time the music slows down, we're both dripping with sweat, and I'm grateful when Peter suggests we get something to drink.

For the first slow song, we watch the others couple up, then I see Stephanie and her date head out to the floor. She waves and smiles. I wave back.

No way am I ready to press my body against Peter's. Just holding hands on the limo ride almost made me lose my breath. I'd rather be pegged as a lesbian, a loser, a priss, anything—I just don't want to terminally embarrass myself by passing out or having a heart attack. And a part of me keeps wondering, why me? Why did Peter pick me? And is he going to try to kiss me?

Dr. Max always warned me to be careful with kisses, because one can lead to more, but I sense that though Peter acts cool and all together, deep down even he's a little scared. Could he be gay and not know it yet? Would he freak if he knew about me?

Around us, everyone seems to be touching.

Bryce Swenson glares at Peter over some girl's shoulder. Catching Peter's eye, Bryce reaches down and squeezes the girl's butt as if he owns her. The girl squeals but doesn't push him away. Peter looks sad, shakes his head. "Can you keep a secret?" he whispers. He's watching Bryce. "She's my ex," he nods in their direction, and then turns toward the drink table. "We went out for two years, but our dads hated each other." His eyes get watery and I look away, saving us both. "A Romeo and Juliet kind of thing," he says.

I look back, but now her head's buried in Bryce's chest. "Do you miss her?" I ask.

"At first. That's what sort of started all the rumors." He shakes his head again.

"Rumors?" That he's gay or his dad's a Mafia-kingpin murderer? I want him to say more, but he spots Joel and never answers.

Peter takes my hand, leading me in the direction of Joel and Roslyn. An image of his perfect lips kissing mine flickers through my mind.

I've never really kissed anyone.

Except Sarah Shorter, back in Berkeley, when I was ten. She was twelve. She tasted like grape gum, and I gagged when she stuck her tongue in my mouth, even though I wanted to keep going. She said I had to kiss her because she'd bet someone she could kiss every guy at school. We had to stop because Mr. Shorter came whizzing up the alley on his motor scooter. Never happened again, but it wasn't because I didn't think about it.

A lot.


Joel and Roslyn are waiting for us at the other end of the refreshment table. Joel glances around and quickly pours something into a paper cup. Roslyn clings to his arm.

Joel comes up and offers the cup to me. I shake my head. Just smelling the booze makes me dizzy.

He then offers the cup to Peter. Peter laughs and takes a swig. "Hey, Alyx, a little won't hurt. We have a driver."

"I hafta go to the bafroom," Roslyn mumbles, her face suddenly pale.

Joel hands her arm to me and we hurry from the gym, avoiding Mr. Wexler, who's boring some kids in the hallway with stories of his old glory days.

"How much did you drink?" I say quietly, but Roslyn only closes her eyes. I want to lecture her, to remind her about the girl that ended up dead in a ditch that Coach told us about, but instead, I push open a stall door with my foot and lean away just in time.

The acidy smell of her vomit turns my stomach.

"Roslyn?"

Pushing me away, she locks herself in the stall. I stand outside listening to her gulp for breath when the door to the restroom swings open.

"Hey, Alyx," Stephanie says, all perky. "Peter's peer pressure finally got you, hey?"

I smile and turn on the faucet full blast so Stephanie won't hear Roslyn in the stall behind us.

Stephanie preens in the mirror, tucking a strand of blond hair behind her ear. The rest of it tumbles around her shoulders. I have mine pulled back in a kind of makeshift French knot, though it's barely long enough and it needed a ton of product to stay in place.

Even though the water's still on full blast, I notice that Roslyn's suddenly stone silent.

Barely able to look at my reflection, I pretend to check my mascara as Stephanie offers me a tube of frosted lip gloss. "Want some? It tastes awesome."

Leaving the water running, I apply a generous coat to my lips and hand it back. "Like cherries."

"Yeah, don't you love it?" She reaches over and touches my dress. "Wow, Alyx—this is gorgeous on you!" Suddenly, she makes a face. "Does it reek in here or what?"

Behind us, Roslyn tries to muffle a cough.

"Oh, my God!" Stephanie giggles. "Someone's in here?"

"I'm waiting on Roslyn." I motion behind us. The principal's daughter doesn't need to know that Roslyn is wasted, or that Joel and Peter are well on their way. If her dad found out, our team could kiss any chance at State good-bye. And it's practically a guarantee that Stephanie has not been drinking, so I pray Roslyn stays where she is so Stephanie doesn't associate the awful smell with her.

Finally, Stephanie leaves, and I hear Roslyn's hoarse voice. "Is she gone?"

"Yeah."

I'm furious when Roslyn emerges.

"Don't you think Stephanie could smell you a mile off? What if you get caught?"

Roslyn examines her reflection in the mirror. She's a little less pale at least.

"Come on, Alyx, it's like sooo yesterday. Let's just have fun."

"You call puking your guts out—"

Joel's muffled voice comes through the door. "Ladies, your limo awaits. We have another party to attend."

I look at Roslyn. "Party?"

Roslyn hiccups. "Remember? Pepper and Clay's, at the Pitmanis'."

I'd forgotten.

## CHAPTER 31

# Double Exposure

By the time we're back in the limo, my mind is mining through a million different excuses to get out of this stupid party.

"I have a curfew," I protest as we pull out of the parking lot.

Peter grins. His eyes look glassy now, too. "Don't worry, Alyx. We're only across the park, and I'll walk you home by midnight." His arm slides behind me on the seat. "If Pepper acts like a pain, I'll deal with her. I'm used to it."

Feeling his hand on my back, I freeze. I don't mean to; it just happens, and he removes it, acts all casual, and leans in, explaining gently, "She doesn't mean to be such a pain. Sometimes she gets this crazy idea she's okay without her medicine. *Not.*" Then he takes out his phone and checks his texts.

I press my hot face on the cool window glass. I want to ask what the hell is the matter with her, and how come Peter turned out so nice when Pepper is so cruel, but I don't.

Instead, I decide to make a dash for home as soon as we get to the Pitmanis' house.

"Hey, want to see something cool?" Peter offers up his phone.

I nod, take it, and look. On the screen is a photo of a double rainbow arching right over the Harbor Street Bridge, the slate-gray surface of Lake Michigan in the background.

"Took it with my new forty-five millimeter digital. I'll show you when we get home. I can't bring that one to school 'cause Dad would kill me if something happened to it. It shoots fifty frames a minute, and the shudder speed's unbelievable."

I haven't a clue what he's taking about. As he chatters away, a strange memory of Prickman pops into my brain and I find myself half-listening to Peter while thinking about the time Prickman and his pals spray-painted No FAGGOTS ALLOUD on the back wall of the 7-Eleven. Other taggers, better spellers, began adding to it: No FUDGE-PACKERS. No HUMPING HOMOS. QUEERS—SHOT ON SITE. SPONSORED BY THE NRA—No RENAL ASS SEX.

"So when the light refracts through the water, the vapor rises—" Peter's explaining the science behind double rainbows when Joel shouts, "PARTY TIME! WE'RE HERE!" into Roslyn's ear.

Roslyn waves her hand groggily. She's so out of it, it's scaring me. Quickly, I try to sort out the best excuse to ditch them all and head home. I'll just say I'm tired or I don't feel well or I have to get up super early. The limo comes to a complete stop, the door swings open, a gust of frigid air rushes in, and if I'm going to make a dash, I'll need to act fast.

Heavy metal music booms from the inside the house.

"They're down in the pool room," Peter tells Joel and Roslyn as we get out of the limo. "You guys go on down. I wanna show Alyx my new forty-five millimeter first."

I crawl out of the limo, careful not to bunch up my dress or bump my head. The cold air whips through my coat, making me feel naked. The wind smells of tannery smoke and rotting carcass. I look over at the Polish Palace. It feels like its a million miles away. I'd have to run through the park and six inches of slushy snow to get there.

I can see Mom's light on in her attic. Grizzly's basement windows are dark, but Grandpa must still be up, or asleep in his chair, because the TV's light is flickering through a crack in the living room curtains.

An uneasy feeling has settled in my gut and my legs are jumpy, ready to run.

"Come on, Alyx, it'll be okay. It'll be fun!" Roslyn nudges me. She's coming back into herself but still . . . she wobbles on her heels, catches herself, and smiles.

I'm not reassured.

Cars are parked along the driveway and on both sides of the street. I look down at my shoes. My feet are numb. Against every instinct, I nod, and when Peter squeezes my hand, I let him steer me inside. He piles our coats on a leather bench in the front hall.

Roslyn and Joel stumble down the stairs, laughing. Joel's holding another bottle of something he opened in the car.

I'm trembling.

"Where's Pepper?" I try to not to sound paranoid.

"Come on." He takes my hand and leads me into a huge wood-paneled office. The walls are covered with oil paintings. The boom from the speaker downstairs vibrates the floor beneath us. "This is Dad's den. He's obsessed with Baroque Italian art." Peter waves his hand as he leads me across the room and opens an ornate paneled door. "And here's Dad's darkroom."

I stop just inside the door. Take my hand back. "Should we be in here?" My throat's like sandpaper.

He ignores my question, reaches over, and slowly spins me toward him. The heavy door closes behind us. Dimmed florescent bulbs cast a greenish light over counters piled high with cameras, computers, and various parts. Dozens of photos hang from a laundry line that runs from one end of the room to the other.

"I come here when I can't stand my life anymore," Peter whispers. One of his hands is on my arm; the other he slides around my waist.

My eyes scan the room. Most of the pictures are of people's faces: some superimposed on others, some clear, and some fuzzy around the edges. "He builds and designs security equipment," Peter nods at the photos. "Those are from a security camera that can take your face-print, just like a finger print."

I flash back to Pepper explaining how she found Stephanie's grade school photo.

*Does he have photos of me in here?*

He leans toward me, almost like he's going to kiss me, and now, I feel both of his hands resting lightly on my hips. He must feel me trembling.

"I like you, Alyx. You're not like other girls," he says.

I pull away and try to laugh. "What'd you mean?"

He shrugs, drops his arms, and laughs, too. "Well, you're taller for one thing." Not looking at me, he reaches behind him and takes a camera off a shelf. "You don't talk my ear off. And when you shot that basket at the wrong hoop and shook it off," he looks down into the camera lens still talking, "well . . . you were so cool. I wish I could be like you."

He takes a picture of his shoe. The flash blinds me for a moment. I watch him, remembering that night—how I wanted to crawl in a hole and die. I want to say something, anything, but nothing comes out.

He smiles and then points the camera at my shoes.

I push it away. "I hate having my picture taken."

He looks surprised and lowers the camera. I see his eyes water and it looks like he's about to cry. "Am I too much of a nerd for you?" he spouts.

"No," I say quickly. "It's me. I don't know why, but I always *hated* having my picture taken. You don't have any pictures of me in here do you?" I look around.

He shakes his head and points the camera at the ceiling, talking into the air. "Is it the rumors about Dad? Or me? They aren't true, you know."

Being in this room is starting to creep me out.

"My dad's not really in the mob if that's what you're *worried* about."

"It's not tha—" I start to say, but he keeps going.

"Mom hurt him bad, and Pepper and I are all he's got. That, and a bottle of scotch, or whatever latest thing he's obsessed with." Still looking through the lens at the ceiling, Peter starts playing with the aperture while talking. "And, well, I'm pretty much a disappointment to him. Even though I don't go ballistic like Pepper, at least she's into sports."

The camera clicks a few times and he lets it drop from his eye again. His tears catch me off guard and, without even thinking, I put my hand on his. He looks up and smiles. The smell of stale beer and musty papers makes me light-headed.

"Alyx, I want you to know, I—"

"*Dad's gonna kill you!*" We both jump as Pepper blasts through the door, red-faced and furious. She's holding a glass in her hand, her eyes on fire. "No one's supposed to be in here!"

Peter jumps up, firmly planting himself in front of Pepper. He's holding the camera like a shield. "I'm just showing her my camera."

He's pissed now, too, and I cringe, backing away from both of them.

"Yeah, right." Pepper winks at me and takes a long calculating drink from her glass. The ice clinks. Now the musty room smells like a bar. She pushes past Peter and focuses her attention on me.

"Alyx," she offers me her glass, "want a sip? Coach'll never know, unless someone narcs."

Peter attempts to block her again with his body. "Leave her alone. She's my date, remember?" He glances at me.

I want to run, but Pepper's blocking the door. She flicks her hand and laughs, "It's only soda." Then I hear a sort of strategic softening in her voice. "Are you kidding me? I'm not going to let down our team. Come on downstairs. Don't be antisocial."

Her earnestness sounds calculated—too calm, too fast.

Peter carefully puts down the camera. I watch him. Paralyzed. He looks at his sister. They both seem scared, angry, and not sure what to do.

"Patti—"

"I'm fine, little brother. It really is *only* soda." Pepper smiles a sweet, sly smile as she opens the door. "Come on, the party's a blast!" Light pours in from behind her. "Join us."

Peter takes my hand and leads me downstairs. I can't speak. Protest. Anything. The cavernous room is filled with sounds. Music vibrates from the walls. There's an enormous pool table surrounded by kids from Cudahy, bodies draped over furniture, others sprawled on the floor. I see Joel and Roslyn sitting crosslegged in a circle watching a brown bottle spin.

It points to Roslyn. "Okay. Okay. My turn!"

"Truth or dare!" Everyone chants.

Someone yanks me down to join them. Peter drops beside me. Pepper smiles slyly, and folding her legs under her dress, she sits down next to Joel, who shifts to make room.

"Alyx!" Roslyn screeches, reaching over to hug me.

"Go." Joel nudges Roslyn. He's wearing swim trunks and a tie now.

"I am!" She pauses, then points to Peter. "Dare."

Peter smiles, throws up his hands like he's surrendering. Everyone laughs. I sigh, grateful she didn't point at me. Everything in me wants to run, but I can't seem to make a move.

"Make him take off his pants, too!" Joel laughs.

"Kiss Alyx!" Roslyn blurts.

Everyone laughs, and someone calls, "Lick Alicks, too!"
More laughter.

"Lick Alicks, lick Alicks, lick Alicks!"

Peter smiles and throws his hands up again in a gesture suggestion: "I can't do it."

"Okay, French kiss her," Roslyn squeals.

"Dare! Dare! Dare!" everyone begins to chorus.

My hands fly up to my face as laugher explodes around us.
Joel shouts, "She's shy!"

Peels of laughter erupt around us, and I close my eyes, feeling the heat of Peter as he leans closer. I smell him. Musky. Minty. Sweet. Boy smells. Booze on his breath. Peter's lips press against my hand, where my lips should be. He makes a gross sucking sound. More laughter. My hand is wet from his tongue, and when he pulls away, I let my hands drop to my lap, then his lips zoom in and touch mine for real, and a zip of electricity shoots through me. Suddenly, I start laughing, too, until I see Pepper, over Peter's shoulder, shooting me a dangerous dagger-like look.

*Screw her!* She's the one who wanted me to ask Peter to this stupid dance in the first place! I close my eyes and kiss Peter back. Hard. Passionately. And then we're all tongue on tongue, and I hear hoots and whistles and kids hollering all around us, until someone yells, "She doesn't look too shy to me!" And Peter pulls away, a huge grin smeared across his face. He reaches down, placing his hand in mine. It's slick with sweat. Our fingers intertwine. I don't let myself look at Pepper, but just hang on to Peter, feeling oddly victorious.

The bottle spins three more times before it points to Pepper.

She aims a trigger finger at me, lowers her voice, and says, "Truth."

Peter gives my hand a light squeeze.

I make myself breathe. *I can do this. I can.*

"Truth. Truth. Truth," the group chants, growing louder.

"Alyx, is the editor of the honors biology text, Dr. Avery Zane Atlas, your dad?"

"What? No way!" Peter's head whips around, and he looks at me, surprised. "Seriously?"

Joel laughs. "I don't think sooo!"

Roslyn looks at Pepper, then me. She looks worried suddenly. My brain shifts into overdrive. Why's Pepper asking me *this*? Everybody quiets, waiting for my answer. Slowly, my head starts to nod on its own.

"See, I told you." Pepper jabs Peter with her elbow. All the pretend friendliness disappears when she says, "So, you're his only *son*?"

There's a noose around my neck and I gulp for air.

Peter and Roslyn look perplexed. Everyone stares.

"Google it." Pepper shrugs, stands up, and starts to walk away. Then she stops, turns, and looks directly at me. "Oh and I friended your surfer-buddy, Dylan. He says to say *Hi, Dude.*"

"What the hell, Pepper!" Roslyn jumps in, but Pepper's eyes flash at me.

"Were you gonna tell him?" She nods her head toward Peter. "Or keep lying about who you really are?"

"Tell me what?" Peter looks from me to Pepper.

Pepper licks her lips. An evil smile spreads across her face. "*The truth.*"

It feels like someone just sucker-punched my throat. I can't breath. "I need to go," my voice squeaks, and I leap up, heading for the stairs.

I hear Pepper say behind me, "I know the *truth* about you."

"Wait . . . Alyx." Peter jumps up to follow me. "I'll walk you home."

Tears blind my eyes. All the way to the Polish Palace, Peter keeps talking, apologizing for Pepper's behavior, asking me what's wrong, but all I hear is Pepper's words stampeding through my brain: *the truth about you . . . the truth about you . . . the truth.*

## CHAPTER 32

# Grounded

When I wake up the next morning, it's light outside. I'm home, in my own bed, dressed in my orange and black Cougar sweats. My stomach's a mess and my mouth tastes like I've been sucking on copper pennies. Q fish is swimming near the top of the tank. Looking for breakfast, no doubt.

I listen for Mom or Grandpa. The house is quiet. Mom probably took Grandpa to church. I whisper to Q fish, "Should've listened to Grizzly."

Millions of slivered memories from last night's events unfold in my brain.

*I know the truth about you, I know . . .*

Did Pepper paste it all over Facebook already? I think about Dad and wonder if maybe death *is* a better deal.

Why didn't I change my full name? How'd she find out about Dad and me? Did she find any pictures from my past—maybe the team photos from Valley League? My old yearbook? Dad's obituary? And how did she hook up with Dylan? The jerk hasn't even emailed me in three months. Why would he tell her about me?

I get up and shuffle into the bathroom where my dress is laying in a corner, balled up with my underwear. I splash water on my face without looking at myself in the mirror and hobble back to bed, burying myself under Grandma Clara's quilt. Blocking out the light.

Mom only comes in once the whole day. She's pissed and tells me I'm grounded for breaking curfew. I don't bother to ask when I actually got home, or for how long I'll be grounded, because I'm glad. As far as I'm concerned, never leaving this room again is fine by me.

Ever.

# CHAPTER 33

# Monkettes

I manage to get through the next two weeks of school without speaking to anyone, except twice. Once is in Mr. Anderson's class to answer a question about DNA strands. And the other is today, before practice, when Coach hands out basketballs for winter break.

"Can I have the one from our first game?" I ask quietly, not wanting the others lined up behind to hear.

She waves me into her office while she searches the bottom of a bulging bag. We are now 10–0, undefeated, and expected to stay that way. According to Coach, winter vacation means extra practice time. She fishes out a ball, examines it, and hands it to me. "This is it."

"Thanks." I take the ball and turn to leave.

"Oh, Alyx—"

I stop and turn around. Coach holds out a marker. "It's yours."

"For keeps?"

She nods. "Put your name on it."

"I brought music, Coach!" MJ hollers from somewhere in back of the line.

I take the marker and sign ALYX on the ball.

"I hear you, MJ." Coach laughs and smiles at me. "Alyx, you love basketball, don't you?" She takes the marker back and stares up at me. I don't know what to say.

"You know, I want you girls to have a little fun, too."

*Fun.* I think about Pepper's party. A chill runs up my back.

"Sometimes you're so somber," she says, studying me.

I turn the ball over in my hands, tracing my name with my finger. She goes behind her desk, lifts a boom box off the floor, and hands it to me.

"Find a plug in there and set this up for MJ, would you? We're going to have some fun with practice today. "

I grab the handle and head for the gym. As I pass the line of waiting girls, MJ slaps a CD in my hand.

"Turn it up," she orders.

When I get into the gym, Pepper breezes by silently on her way to the locker room. She's running late. She looks away when I glance up. She's been acting like I don't exist, and, thank God, Peter's making himself scarce, too.

It occurs to me that perhaps Pepper's waiting until after basketball season ends before she ruins my life forever.

As the other girls trickle into the gym, I spy Roslyn. She acts like we're still great friends, like she doesn't even know what Pepper was insinuating the night of the party. She joins me under the basket, shooting and yakking, until Coach tells her to shoot the ball more than her mouth.

Our schedule's been jam-packed. We're averaging two games a week and even though it's been tense on the bus and in the locker room, somehow we manage to pull it together on the court.

We haven't lost yet, in spite of Pepper's refusal to pass me the ball, so why let her ruin the basketball season, too? And this is Coach's last shot at State. She's already announced her retirement, and I'm not going to be the one to let her down. So whether Pepper likes it or not, I'm the only player tall enough to cover the lane, I'm still bringing down more rebounds than anyone else, and I'm tied with her for lead scorer.

Screw her.

After practice, MJ, Martha, and Roslyn block the locker room door, keeping us from leaving.

"Okay, you two." Roslyn's hands are on her hips. "We all know you're not talkin' but what we want to know is why."

I stop and can hear Pepper's breathing behind me.

"Yeah, we aren't leaving until you kiss and make up." Martha waves her hand playfully in Pepper's stony face.

I stand there with my bag slung over my shoulder, the hood of my jacket flipped up, staring at the ground. I shift the ball Coach gave me from one arm to the other.

"Alyx?" Roslyn pokes me, playfully.

"Come on you guys, this place is feeling like a damn monastery." MJ pretends she's praying. "It's like you've turned into a couple of basketball nuns. Taking a vow of silence. What's goin' on?"

Pepper sits down on the bench like a statue, staring straight ahead. She's zombie-like.

Stephanie comes out of the shower, a towel wrapped around her hair. "They'll work it out over break."

"But they haven't talked in two weeks!" Martha locks arms with Roslyn and MJ.

"Let 'em be," Stephanie says.

MJ shrugs and unlocks herself from the arm grid. Martha grabs Roslyn by the waist and drags her out the door. Roslyn waves to me on her way out. "See you at the Y, Alyx!"

Pepper remains frozen to the bench.

I follow MJ outside. It's like stepping into a deep freeze. The cold smacks the breath out of me and my whole body begins to shake. *Why the hell did we move here?*

I lope toward the slush-covered Volkswagen.

Grizzly's traded in his Harley leather for an orange hunter's parka. He glows like an immense sun inside the car. I noticed he's parked right in back of Mr. Pitmani's Mercedes.

It's as cold inside the Sunbug as it is outside. The heat has never worked right.

"Hey," Grizzly says.

"Hey," I say back, Milwaukee-nese for, "Have a good day?"

MJ stands at the corner bus shelter, shuffling from foot to foot, blowing steam from her mouth into her mittens. Grizzly nods at her. "She need a ride?"

I shrug.

"You need a ride?" He hollers out his half-opened window to MJ.

She hops over a snow bank and runs toward us. "Thank you, Jesus! You got room?"

Grizzly orders me to make room. I jump out and squeeze myself into the backseat. The plastic cracks when I sit down. I can feel my hair bumping the ceiling of the car as MJ climbs into the front seat.

"I can sit back there," MJ offers. Her teeth are chattering.

"I'm fine."

MJ turns and grins at me. "She *can* talk!"

Grizzly smiles into the rearview mirror and grunts, "Where to?"

"Division Street. The Ridgebacks. It's a ways—you sure it's okay?"

"Off thirty-second? One of Pitbull's famous palaces?"

MJ laughs. "It's home. At least until I'm a big-time doctor, then I'll be setting up my mama and my brothers in one of those luxury condos on the lake."

Grizzly drives dangerously close to the Mercedes as we pull out.

MJ lives in the dumpiest apartment complex I've ever seen. Beer cans, old tires, and fast food bags litter the front lawn. A group of scruffy looking men are standing around a trash-can burning something. They're surrounded by broken lawn chairs, a bunch of old potbelly grills, and some rusty cars without tires. One wears at least three different jackets and two mismatched hats. He shoves wads of rolled-up newspaper into the can. As MJ runs toward a door, he calls out to her.

She ignores him.

Approaching Grizzly's car window, another guy spits on the windshield. It freezes in a jagged streak and he wipes it with his sleeve. Steam leaks from his nostrils. "Sorry, man. How 'bout I scrape it for a dollar?"

Grizzly rolls down his window. "How 'bout you leave it or I kick your ass?"

The other men laugh. "Ooee. Fat-ass white boy talk!"

The man with the coats smiles slyly. He leans near the window to check me out. "You Mitesha's boyfriend? She been crossin' the tracks?"

I shrink backwards.

"Oh, sorry, Sugar, you's one of them boy-girls, ain't you?" His hand travels to his crotch. He grabs himself, makes a lewd motion with his hips, and puckers his lips. "Old Amos ain't fussy. I like dat candy, too!"

Grizzly swings his door open, knocking the guy away from the car. The man staggers and trips over his own feet. The other men howl with laugher as Grizzly slams the door shut, guns the Sunbug, and drives me home in silence.

I turn my face to the window and press my cheek to the glass so he can't see me crying.

In the driveway, he yanks on the parking brake and looks at me. "Alyx? I'm sorry about that back there."

Inside, I feel something snap and my fist slams against the seat in front of me. "Do I look like a *guy*?"

Grizzly blinks.

"Do I?" I pound the seat again.

"When you're different, you gotta have a thick skin." He shakes his head, disappointed. "Wish I'd had a thicker one with those guys, myself."

"But do I look like a *guy* to you?" My voice comes out loud, forceful.

"Well, it's kind of like being fat," Grizzly starts. "People notice you and some of them stay away because they're afraid. They're afraid it'll rub off on them. With you, Alyx, it's even harder. People sense something's different, only they can't figure out what. They don't know, so they egg you on. Try to make you crack. It's instinctive—a predator kind of thing. They've got to protect their species—it's evolutionary, DNA hard-wired. In all of us."

"Uncle Joe, I'm not having this stupid conversation with you," I yell. "*Fat* is not my species! And even if it was, I wouldn't act all proud about it!"

Grizzly shakes his head again and lets out a huge sigh. "When you're older, you'll figure out what I mean."

"I don't want to figure out you're fat fetish thing—"

Reaching over, Grizzly grabs the arm of my coat, and I try to shake him loose, but he's way too strong. "Listen, kid, I've been down this road, and whether you want it or not, I'm giving you some advice."

"You aren't my frickin' father!" I cover my ears but he yanks my hands down. His face is crimson.

"You saw those guys hanging out at the Ridgeback. No amount of booze or drugs or sex or whatever your game is—even basketball—can take that kind of pain away. It only numbs you a while, until you're too stoned or too tired to fight how much you hate yourself. It comes back at you, like a boomerang, over and over, until you learn to deal."

I squirm in my seat. He holds my wrists. The steam from our bodies begins to fog up the windows. He finally loosens his grip. I snap my arms free. Fuming. Not looking at him.

"You're right, Alyx. Maybe I've got a fat fetish, as you call it, but at least I know I'm different. You're different, too. It's the way it is. So you damn well better get used to it."

## CHAPTER 34

# Winter Break

Roslyn is in New York for Hanukkah, and the only person from school I'll even consider talking with on the phone is MJ. She gives me a call one day during the break to try to convince me to come practice at the Y.

"Alyx, what're you trying to prove?" she asks.

I'm avoiding the whole Y scene, lying on my bed, watching Q fish swim laps. I practically feel MJ's finger jabbing me through the phone.

"We need you, girl. You've gotta quit this pouting business, you hear me? You might think you can take your sweet-ass time. But I'm only gonna be a senior once—me, and a few of the others. And how about Coach? She's been at this longer than we've been alive. So knock it off! You hear?"

I loop the tangled black cord around my fingers.

"Alyx, I know you're there. I hear you breathin'. You don't show up at the Y tomorrow, I'm gonna come over to that big old house of yours and drag you're butt outta there."

"The Y's closed tomorrow," I say placidly.

Tomorrow is Christmas day. I untangle myself from the cord and trace my finger up and down the tank. Q fish follows it.

"Alyx, you think I like playing with Pepper Pitmani? I've been kissin' that spoiled white girl's you-know-what for four years, and I'll tell you one thing: she's not gonna change." MJ pauses. "Trust me. I'm standing with you on this, and I'm not the only one. All of us have been playing with Pepper for four years. You don't think we know her game?" Her voice gets louder, so I push the phone farther down on the bed. "Everyone's been where you are now, only you've given her more of a run for her money than any of us ever could. So you're wearin' the bull's-eye, but that doesn't mean you can up and quit on us. We need you, and you've got to stop thinking about yourself and start thinking about the team!"

The sound of Grandpa's Christmas polka album floats in through the door, which is cracked open because of the phone cord.

"You don't do nothin' but breathe into this phone. I'm hangin' up."

*Click.*

I pick up the receiver, put it back on the phone, and drag it with its twisted cord back into the living room. Mom, Grizzly, and Grandpa are stringing popcorn and cranberries as a garland for the tree. As I sit down, Mom reaches over, pulls me toward her, then kisses the top of my head.

"Look at this fabulous mop." She tousles my hair. "Help us, Alyx. I'll get the other bowl."

Grizzly hands me the needle he just started. "Two berries work better than one," he says gruffly, not looking up.

We haven't really spoken to each other since the big blow-out in the car.

Grandpa pushes two cranberries on his string. Then he looks up at me, his eyes magnified by his glasses. "You know, your Grandma Clara had hair like that. Wore it longish, too."

Waving his needle in the air, he calls to Mom, who's headed for the kitchen with a spring in her step. At least this move's been good for *her*.

"Bring Alyx the fresh stuff—it's easier to thread. This stuff keeps crumbling in my hands." His head nods back and forth to the polka beat as he shoves the needle through a piece of popcorn and grins. "'Bout time you learn a few Kowalski traditions."

Grizzly's dragged an enormous tree up the back steps. He chopped off the top two feet to get it to fit under the ceiling. It looks more like an overgrown bush once it's placed in the room.

Suddenly, my throat feels scratchy, and I sneeze.

"Gesundheit," Grandpa says, without losing his concentration. Grizzly says nothing. Mom calls from the kitchen, "I'll turn the heat up."

I pick up a cranberry and squish it down on the needle, thinking that all I want for Christmas is to never have to go back to school. Any school. Ever.

I want to tell Mom about what's been going on, but I don't want her to get all hyped up around the holidays. Besides, what's left for us to do? Milwaukee was supposed to be our fresh start, my big cure. It was supposed to be easier for both of us here.

Mom comes bouncing back in the room with a huge fresh bowl of popcorn. I fake a smile, set it in my lap, and start stringing along with Grandpa and Grizzly, fighting off the sense of hopelessness sneaking in around the edge of my consciousness.

CHAPTER 35

# Unfriended

I've already wrapped Mom's present and put it under the tree, with a few small things that are piled up, mostly marked for me.

Mom opens her gift first. It's the ball Coach gave me. I'd washed it with Dove soap in the bathroom sink, dried it with a bath towel, and written under my autograph, in indelible ink: *To Mom, my biggest fan no matter which basket I shoot at!*

Breaking down in sobs, she hugs me and the ball. When she finally lets go, Grizzly grabs the ball and spins it on his finger until she grabs it back. "Just like the old days," Grandpa complains to Grizzly. "Stop annoying your sister!"

Grizzly giggles.

My gifts include a scarf—in Cougar colors—from Grandpa. He made it himself from a ball of orange-and-black yarn I'd seen circulating around the house.

"When you go to State, he wants you to stay warm in style." Mom gets up and gives Grandpa a hug. I get up, too, thank him, and lean over to give him a hug. He's surprisingly boney and small as my arms wrap around him and I realize it's the first time since we arrived that I've actually touched him.

Grizzly leans over, yanks the scarf from my neck, and wraps it around his own. "No fair. I want one, too, Pops!"

Everyone laughs.

Grandpa grabs hold of my hand, smiles, and squeezes it gently. "Don't you let your uncle or anyone else pick on you—you hear?"

I'm trying not to think about school and Pepper, but it's next to impossible.

My next gift is the size of a glove box. When I pick it up, Mom comes and kneels next to me. "This is from me and your uncle. We got a super deal. The other one goes with it. You can open that later."

Grizzly shrugs at Grandpa like he doesn't know what's inside.

I peel away the paper to reveal a shiny new phone.

"Wow, thanks," is all I can say. Kowalski tradition usually means you can only give gifts that are homemade or cost less than thirty dollars. Mom and Grizzly definitely broke the rules. Grandpa looks confused.

"It's a smartphone, Pops," Grizzly explains. "It slices and dices, and now she can do Facebook, emails, and stay connected to everybody and everything."

Grandpa shakes his head. "At least it's not some damn meat-eating fish!"

Then I peek inside the envelope. A phone plan, one year, prepaid. Not that I have anyone to call.

When everyone starts singing Christmas carols, I thank them for the gifts and go up to my room. Q fish rushes to the side of the tank to greet me, her loyalty still intact. I sit down on my bed and toss the phone at my feet. Peter's been trying to email me over the holiday, but I've been deleting each message without reading it. I don't want to know what's being said about me either online or via text.

I look at Q fish. She blows bubbles from her tiny lips. "I. Don't. Want. To. Know," I tell her, and she seems to understand. With my foot, I shove the smartphone off the edge of my bed and it clunks onto the floor.

CHAPTER 36

# Baby Jock of the Week

My first day back, in homeroom, I open the *Cudahy Courier* to read:

COUGAR GIRLS GO TO STATE!

*The Cudahy Lady Cougars will be a prime contender as they head to the State Tournament for the first time in twenty-three years. Senior point guard, Stephanie Wexler, is confident the Lady Cougars can bring home the Big Cup.*

*Coach Carol Chance, with a 20–0 record under her belt, cautioned that anything can happen at tournament time. She says the critical thing for this team to remember is that every game is a new game. "If these girls can stick to fundamentals and play team ball, they have an excellent chance of locking up the State tournament."*

*She's warned her Lady Cougars that over the years she's witnessed countless underdogs upset the status quo.*

*"In a way, we are the underdogs, coming back after twenty-three dry years. The pressure is on for us to finish out strong, but I believe my girls are up to the challenge."*

Below the article, a highlighted box reads: ATHLETE OF THE WEEK. I stare at it and my stomach drops like I just stepped off the edge of the Grand Canyon.

It's about me.

Freefalling, my head is all fuzzy and I'm trying to figure out what to do before I hit the ground. There's a picture of five-year-old me with a boy buzz cut. Dylan's standing next to me with his long-flowing hippie curls, wearing a tie-dyed T-shirt. I'm in Batman pajamas and a sequined blue cape. The caption reads: *Cudahy High baby jock of the week, Alyx Kowalski, is on the right.*

Frantically, I look around the room. A school paper sits on every desk. Bryce Swenson steps through the door, slides into his seat, and puts his head down on the desktop, not bothering to look at the paper.

*It's only a matter of time. Collect them. Burn them!*

My mind races in circles. The article's author is listed as "staff." I can't stop myself from looking at it. The article sums up my season, stating I'm only a sophomore, but a leading scorer. It quotes Coach:

*"Alyx has one of the best turn-around jump shots at the Regional level. She's become a quiet leader in the Lady Cougars' forward line up."*

*Known by friends to be shy by nature, Alyx declined a personal interview. We can tell you that Alyx was born in California, grew up in Berkeley, and later moved to Bakersfield. According to the Walnut Grove Middle School yearbook, Alyx played in the Walnut Grove Valley League, aspiring to someday play in the NBA and outscore Laker legend Kobe Bryant. Lucky for the Lady Cougars, Alyx is following fast in his footsteps. We look forward to seeing more of Alyx Kowalski as the Lady Cougars head to State.*

Not that bad. My heart's thumping like someone's taken a sledgehammer to my chest. *Breathe, Alyx.* Kids file in around me, sitting down in their seats. The old panic is pushing into my brain and my feet are itching to run.

A girl named Tracy Allen points at the picture and smiles at me. I shoot her back a lame smile and then put my head down on the desk. I want to cry, hide, and scream all at the same time.

How did Pepper get that picture? No pronouns, except Coach's quote. Does she know now? She has to. I should have just given her the stupid interview!

Roslyn's waiting for me outside homeroom. I fly past her to my locker.

She races after me. "Alyx! Man alive! What's up? Like, hello, I haven't seen you in weeks. Aren't you going to talk to me?"

I look straight ahead, the pounding of my heart hurdling me forward.

"Okay, then, I'll talk to you." She trails after me. "Holiday break back in New York was a total bust. My cousin—"

I'm shoving books into my backpack.

"Hey, what's the matter?"

I slap the school paper into her hand, and she glances at it.

"I already saw it." She looks down at the paper and then back up at me. "What's the big deal? Pepper just wants to go to State. MJ and Stephanie talked to her. She's not going to mess with you anymore."

I slam my locker shut. "You don't know the half of it, Roslyn!" I snap my finger against the picture. "Where'd she get this?"

Roslyn throws up her hands, "Jeez, how would I know?" She looks more closely and points at five-year-old me. "How adorable. Is that your brother?"

My eyes fill with angry tears.

"I don't get why you're so upset. Who cares, anyway?"

"*I* do!" Shoving my arms into my jacket, I fling my backpack over my shoulder.

"Okay, okay, don't spazz out about it. Hey, where're you going?"

Roslyn's voice trails after me down the hall. She sounds desperate, "If we get detention, Coach'll kill us. Alyx!"

As if on cue, Mr. Wexler turns the corner and Roslyn shoves me into the girls bathroom, where I bury my face in my hands, sobbing. She tries to puts her arms around me, but I push her away.

The door opens and Mr. Wexler pops his head in. He glances up and down the hall and then furrows his eyebrows. Seeing that I'm crying, he looks concerned.

"She's a little upset, Mr. Wexler," Roslyn states the obvious.

"Well," he clears his throat, "please get to class." He stands aside as Roslyn grabs my arm and we brush past him.

"Roslyn," I beg when we're out of Wexler's sight, "don't be mad at—"

She grabs my arms. "OMG! Alyx, we just lucked out like mega-big time." She pushes me in the direction of Mr. Anderson's class. "See you at practice!"

## CHAPTER 37

# Nowhere to Run

After school, I grab my gym bag and head for the locker room. Only two kids even mentioned the article today. I'm starting to feel better until I see MJ and Stephanie standing outside the locker room.

"You best know, girl," MJ points, looking a little worried. "There's a party goin' on in there, and I think it's for you."

"My dad's in there with Roslyn and Coach," Stephanie speaks softly. She looks scared and there's a warning tone to her voice. "Your mom and your uncle are there, too. Coach told us to send you in."

I am frozen in place.

MJ's shaking her head. "Why does this team always land a girl who can't keep her butt outta trouble?"

Gently, Stephanie takes my arm and tries to lead me toward the door. "Better see what's up."

But I whirl around and start walking the other way. Breaking into a sprint, I propel myself through the front doors into the

207

freezing air, where a line of idling school buses snakes around the corner. I dodge through clouds of white exhaust and jump onto bus seventy-eight, tumbling into the back seat where I duck down low. None of the other kids look at me, and I sink into the seat, shivering.

Then I hear Stephanie shout, "She's on one of 'em."

I close my eyes.

"Alyx?"

It's Grizzly. A kid in front turns in terror and points at me.

The bus sways back and forth as he lumbers down the narrow aisle toward me, wearing his orange parka and looking like a grounded Goodyear blimp.

I squeeze my eyes, tight.

*God, no!*

Then I hear his strained breathing beside me. "We're goin' in to find out what this is about."

It's too late to fight back. I open my eyes and stand up, resigned to my fate. No one laughs as we get off—no one makes a peep—and I follow him back to the locker room.

The sea of girls lined up outside parts for Grizzly like he's some huge motorcycle Moses on an urgent mission.

In Coach's office, Mom gives me a hug. I refuse the seat she offers. My teeth are chattering. Roslyn's face is wet with tears. Coach asks her to leave. We avoid each other's eyes. Mr. Wexler's leaning against Coach's desk. He's so pale that he looks like a standing corpse. A letter dangles from his fingers.

Grizzly's usual labored breathing surprisingly calms me as Mom takes the letter from him.

"Alyx, it seems that someone has raised a few questions and I've had to explain a few things to both your coach and Mr. Wexler. I told Coach Chance and Mr. Wexler that you have a right to know about this," Mom says.

I swallow hard. I must have bitten my cheek at some point because my mouth tastes like blood. *Know about what?*

"Carol and I will step out for a minute," Wexler clears his throat. "I'm not concerned about you missing a few minutes of class today, Alyx. It seems we have a bigger problem on our hands."

Mom puts her arm around me as they step outside the office, and I take the letter from Mom's grasp. It's from the Interscholastic Sports Commissioner. Grizzly peers over my shoulder as I read it aloud:

*Dear Mr. Wexler:*

*It has come to my attention that a Lady Cougar by the name of Alyx Kowalski may be misrepresenting herself. As you know, the Wisconsin Interscholastic Athletic Association must ensure that all athletes compete in a healthy and fair manner. The issue in question is that Ms. Kowalski's previous school records list her gender as male under the surname Atlas. However, her current records register her as female.*

*As you know, the reason we separate the girls from the boys is to create equality and safety in competition. If Ms. Kowalski has represented herself as a female athlete when she is, in fact, a male, we will be forced to disqualify the Lady Cougars from further interscholastic competition on the State tournament level.*

*Although it seems unfair to penalize the entire team, it is also unfair to the other teams who didn't qualify for the State competition because they competed against a team harboring an ineligible player. If Ms. Kowalski is a boy, she must play on a boys team.*

*I have reviewed the records and statistics and it would seem she is an accomplished athlete. I do not want to jump to conclusions. So I ask that you provide evidence of Ms. Kowalski's gender within the week. I suggest you request a routine physical examination from the enclosed list of approved physicians. Without such evidence, I cannot in good conscience permit the team to move on to the State competition level.*

*Thank you for your help in resolving this matter.*
*Very Truly,*
*Joseph Bender, Interscholastic Sports Commissioner*

I ball up the letter in my fist. Mom peels it from my fingers and hands it to Grizzly. Then I notice the school paper lying open to my article on Coach's desk.

Pepper won. She's ruined my life!

"I told your coach and Mr. Wexler," I hear Mom saying, "that Dr. Royce will send whatever proof they need. And I apologized for lying on your school application and saying you we're homeschooled."

Grizzly heaves a big sigh. "Sis, you should've told 'em right away."

Though she looks tough, Mom's voice is quivering. "I thought it was best." She wipes a tear away. "You know as well as I do, Joey—Milwaukee isn't the most accepting place on the planet."

A knock on the glass wall attracts our attention. Coach and Mr. Wexler gesture if they can re-enter. Mom starts to shake her head, but I amaze myself by saying, "Uncle Joe's right."

Dr. Royce's words rush into my head: *"We all have a right and an obligation to be who we are . . . a person's your enemy, Alyx, only if you give them power . . . stand up, look them in the eyes, refuse to carry any shame . . . truth is the mightiest sword."*

I suddenly think about MJ, how she has to face being one of a handful of kids of color at school and how she jokes about being a distraction; and also how she doesn't let where she comes from stop her from dreaming. And Roslyn, too. She just seems to love and accept everybody and she doesn't tolerate abuse or give her power over to anyone. Then there's Grizzly, who takes the teasing about his weight, yet demands respect. And finally, I think about me—how I feel so sorry for myself all the time and how I always want to run. But I know that I can't—not anymore.

Not since the day with Prickman behind the 7-Eleven have I felt this bad, have I wanted to kill myself, have I wished that I'd never been born—like I'm a mistake. But I look over at Mom and Grizzly, and I know no matter how humiliated or terrified or shitty I feel, if this is how Pepper Pitmani's going to take me down, I'm not going down without a fight!

I turn to Coach, who has entered the office with Mr. Wexler. Her jaw tightens. She's holding back tears. Her eyes search mine and I feel her heart breaking for me. She's stood by me—by all of us—over all these months. Trying to get us to understand what it means to be a team. This is her last chance, her last season, the pinnacle of her entire career. But I can see it's not her career she cares about right now. It's me.

With Mom and Grizzly flanking me, and Dr. Royce's words ringing in my ear, I try to look at Mr. Wexler through a glaze of tears. He stares at me, his pinpoint eyes shifting back and forth.

Grizzly squeezes my shoulder. "Like my sister said, the kid's been through enough."

*Look them in the eyes.*

Even though I try to draw strength from them, Dr. Royce's words begin to play tag in my brain, and my entire body starts to tremble. Mom opens her mouth, but I wipe my eyes and jump in, cutting her off: "Coach? Mr. Wexler? Mom told you about me, right?"

*Look them in the eyes.*

They nod.

Mom butts in, "Under the circumstances, I thought it —"

"It's okay." I put up my hand and she stops. I then turn to Coach. "I had one surgery already, and I'll have another when I turn eighteen."

Coach watches me intensely. I try to speak confidently. "No one knows better than I do. This is my team. I am a girl."

A flicker of relief sparks in Coach's eyes. "And one heck of a ball player," she whispers.

Grizzly punches Mr. Wexler in the arm. "Yeah, one heck of a ball player!"

Wexler winces.

Coach looks at her watch. "The girls are waiting to practice."

Mr. Wexler seems lost in thought. "Alyx, it's not that I don't believe you or your family. Only I'm certain Mr. Bender will need some medical evidence." He glances from Mom to me, and stutters, "In addition to this Dr. Royce, perhaps someone local could give us a report this week?" He hesitates, picking up the letter again. "Would you be willing to see one of these doctors?"

Simultaneously, Mom and I say, "No."

"She's seen enough doctors." Mom rubs my back.

I sigh—wishing my life wasn't so damn complicated, wishing I'd been born like other kids, either a boy or a girl and not some strange friggin' abnormality with an extra X chromosome that doesn't quite fit anywhere.

Coach grabs the letter from Wexler. "Jack, for God's sake!"

Wexler spreads his hands. "What do you want me to do? You know the Sports Commissioner better than I do, Carol. Bender's not going to take my word for this, and he's certainly not going to take yours. We need to forge a reasonable response."

Coach slaps the letter onto her desk. "The Commissioner's always been a homophobe, but to go after a student— think about it, Jack." She holds up her hands. "At whose expense are his *religious beliefs* causing harm now?"

"The man's been with the district forever, Carol! What do you suggest I tell him?" Wexler rubs his forehead.

"Well, so have I!" Coach's eyes turn to stone. "Tell the bastard to back off. If you can't, I will!"

Wexler taps his fingers on the desktop, a slow exhale leaks from his lips.

"End this meeting, Jack, so I can get my girls to practice and Alyx can decide for herself what *evidence*, if any, she wants to provide." She picks up the letter, folds it in half, and says to me, "I'll handle the Commissioner, if that's all right with you, Alyx. Your job is to keep your faith in yourself and your team. Okay?"

A shiver shakes through me.

Wexler's face looks strained. "Once we have the facts of this situation straightened out, I hope we can work together to create a more welcoming and . . ." he stumbles around trying to find the right word, "inclusive atmosphere at Cudahy High." He takes a white handkerchief from his back pocket, removes his glasses, and wipes his forehead. "Carol, when you speak to Bender, ask him about the source of this information. His timing, as usual, is uncanny."

Before he walks out the door, Wexler turns to Coach. "The tournament starts Friday. We have exactly four days to get this resolved. And I don't need to remind you that my own daughter is a senior this year. And there will be scouts from three top-ten schools watching."

Coach looks over at me. "Okay, Alyx, suit up. We've taken up enough practice time."

Just then, a series of sneezes overwhelms me.

Coach jiggles the whistle that hangs from her neck. "Let's hope you're not coming down with the same bug Pepper went home with today."

*Yeah, right. I bet Pepper's sick.*

When I sneeze again, Coach says, "Maybe you'd better get home and rest up for Friday." Mom looks worried. Coach flips a tangle of keys from her pocket and escorts us to an emergency exit door. It empties outside so I don't have to confront any of the team.

Mom feels my forehead as we walk. "You're warm," she says in her nurse voice. "Let's get you home." I push her away.

Coach is watching me as she shakes both Mom's and Grizzly's hands. "We'll get it worked out. It would be shame to stop the girls now—we're so close." Then she turns me gently toward her. Her hands are solid, strong, but her voice becomes unusually tender. "Alyx, I know a bit about what you're going through here, and if you've learned anything from me all season, let it be this—don't let *anyone* hold you back from who you are or what you love. You understand me?"

Our eyes meet.

I nod.

She flings the steel door open, waits for us to pass, then pulls it firmly shut behind us.

## CHAPTER 38

# Born That Way

All night my body twitches and sweats with fever and in the morning my throat is so swollen I can barely swallow, let alone talk. When I try to wish good morning to Q fish, the sound of my voice scrapes through my insides. If Pepper really is sick—though I suspect she's faking—I hope her throat swells up so bad it chokes her to death.

I think about Dad and then feel bad for feeling so hateful, but a part of me can't help it.

Around six in the morning, a knock sounds at the door.

I pull Grandma's quilt up over my head.

Mom peaks in, then tiptoes over to the bed. She thinks I'm still asleep, so she leaves after resting her cool hand on my forehead.

A part of me hopes I'm sick enough to die, because I really don't ever want to step foot in Cudahy High again. And even though I get what Coach said about me not selling out, the thought of everybody knowing about me is worse than death.

I wish I could stay home forever. Every day I'd hang with Grizzly and Mom and Grandpa, and we could have our own private circus. Grizzly could dance disco, Grandpa could play fifty million renditions of the Polish National Anthem on his accordion, and Mom could dye her dreadlocks orange and play the part of a clueless clown. And me? Well, I'll be the freak, of course — the half-boy, half-girl sideshow freak.

I check out my reflection in the side of the fish tank.

It's true. Even though inside I feel like a girl and I get a period now and Dr. Royce can make my parts more "authentic" looking, it doesn't matter. None of it does. Once a weirdo, always a weirdo, and the Pepper Pitmanis of the world will always track me down, sniff me out.

Grizzly's right.

Pitbulls can't help what they are. They're born that way.

Just like me.

## CHAPTER 39

# Messages

Without knocking, Grizzly comes into my room around midday to feed the fish.

"Alyx, this filter needs to be cleaned every week." He sounds irritated. "This Goldie looks terrible." He points to Q fish.

"She's fine," I squeak.

"What the hell's wrong with her?"

I sit up and follow Grizzly's finger. Q fish looks the same as ever. Dizzy, I lie back down.

He huffs and looks at me. "You gonna go to their doctor?"

I look away bitterly.

No way am I going to go to *their* stupid doctor. What would it prove anyway? People just don't get that not every damn person on this planet fits into a gender box.

"Sorry, it's not my business," he grumbles. "In case your coach calls, I put the phone outside your door. And I activated your cell." I look over toward the desk where the phone I'd left in the box had disappeared. "Used the same number your mom says you had in California. That way your friends will find you." He pulls the phone from his pocket and holds it up to show me.

*What friends?*

Grizzly looks down at me from the end of the bed and says, "Call me or your mom if you've got any problems, okay? I programmed our numbers in." He tosses the phone on the bed. "The ancient one was up burning the midnight oil again, and your mom doesn't want him exposed to whatever you got." Reaching down, he grabs my toes under the blanket.

For once, I don't pull away.

"Alyx?"

I'm nodding off again. Thinking about Dad. What it must have felt like to lie in a rent-a-bed for three years with a trachea tube shoved down his throat. How did he stand it? It must have been torture.

Shortly after Grizzly leaves, the phone outside the door starts ringing. Grandpa doesn't bother answering it. Either he isn't wearing his hearing aids, or he's asleep in his chair, or both.

Fortunately, no one at school knows I have a cell yet and maybe I'll keep it that way. I lie in bed like a zombie listening to the phone ring until the answering machine picks up.

"Hey, Alyx, this is Stephanie. Coach said you're sick. Just want you to know that me'n the team are hoping you'll be well for State. And hey, get well. We miss ya."

*Click.*

What did Coach tell them? Do they realize the whole team could be disqualified because of me?

*Ring. Ring. Ring.*

"Hi, Honey, just checking in to see how you're feeling. Home by five. I gave your grandpa strict instructions to let you rest. I told him no music. Period. So rest up."

*Click.*

The phone keeps ringing and the messages keep coming.

"Alyx, call me," Roslyn says. "I just want you to know you're my friend no matter what! And call me, like tonight, okay? Because everyone's freaking out and I need to talk to you."

*Click.*

"Alyx, hope you appreciate this. I'm risking my beautiful black ass to check up on you. Peter's letting me use his cell. Mine croaked." MJ laughs. "Rumor is you're really sick, so don't pick this up, just get well. We need you, girl!"

*Click.*

Peter's voice sounds like he's in a tunnel. "This is a message for Alyx. This is Peter. Alyx, check your emails." There's the sound of a toilet flushing. "Gotta go."

*Click.*

Coach's voice booms, "Hello, this is Carol Chance. Alyx, could you or your mother give me a call? I had a conversation with the Sports Commissioner."

*Click.*

"Hello, my name is Jake Millmen. I'm with the *Milwaukee Sentinel* and we'd like to verify a story line for this Tuesday's edition. Would you please have Alyx Kowalski contact us?"

I pull my pillow over my ears. I want to go unplug the thing, but I can't muster the energy to move.

I stare at Q fish while having a feverish conversation in my head: *Did you ever wish you were something else? Like a dog? If you were a dog, you'd be much more useful. You could play fetch. You could retrieve things. You could be my guard dog, growl at jerks, and scare away burglars. You could keep me warm at night. But no, you have to be a useless fish, an ugly, sad, pathetic fish, trapped in your water world.*

I tap on the glass.

*It's just the way it is, right?*

# CHAPTER 40

# Peter Apologizes

It was once standard practice for doctors to take babies like me and make us into girls automatically. Often without telling the parents. They justified that, as girls, our lives would be easier. But that fell out of fashion because of the ones who never got a period or those who started growing beards when they hit puberty. No one knew why until someone searched the kid's medical records or the child was sent to a pediatric endocrinologist, like Dr. Royce—someone used to seeing this kind thing.

I think my life would've definitely been easier if they'd have just "adjusted" me right away, but bummer for me, Dad and Mom were always *ahead of their time.*

They chose to wait, which is now the standard thing to do.

And I'm definitely not alone. Dr. Royce claims 2 percent of the babies born in the United States are gender fluid, or intersex, and many scientists believe there are more than two genders. Dr. Royce once told me the problem with gender identification arises when people try to put their babies into gender boxes that don't fit.

Whatever. It doesn't really work in practice, though. What were my parents supposed to tell people? They were raising an "it"?

Now, it's up to me to clean up the mess.

Should I go to one of their stupid doctors? Why torture myself?

I'm still in bed and know that I can't play with a raw throat, fever, and barely enough energy to get out of bed anyway. Dozing on and off, I try not to think about my problem, until Mom knocks at my door. "Still feeling rough, Honey?"

I nod weakly.

She checks my temperature. "Do you want me to call Coach back for you?"

I nod.

"Your friend Peter's waiting on the porch. Do you want me to bring him up?"

I must look surprised, because Mom adds, "He knows you're not feeling well. Says he'll only stay for a few minutes. It seems kind of urgent."

Pulling Grandma's quilt up around my neck, I shrug, too shocked to deny his request. I'm preparing myself not to believe a word he says. Did he know Pepper was trying to trap me all along? Was he in on it, too?

"Alyx?" Peter steps into my bedroom. There's no camera around his neck, and he's holding a card in his hand. I hear Mom's footsteps retreat down the hallway.

He nods at the desk chair. "Can I sit?"

I stare at him and narrow my eyes suspiciously.

He stays standing, turning the card over in his hands.

"Listen, Alyx. I came to tell you I'm sorry about the Truth or Dare game. What Pepper did was really mean." With one hand, he runs his fingers through his hair.

My body shivers under the quilt.

"I told my dad what happened that night. I mean, everything. The party. The booze." Peter swallows a huge breath. "When he got home, Pepper tried to deny it and she expected me to cover for her as usual, but I'd already told him so she broke down and confessed." He crosses the room and lays the card on the end of the bed. "It's from her. She's barricaded herself in her room. She's not talking to me, but Dad asked me to bring this over."

I open the envelope. The card inside has a butterfly on the cover.

*Dear Alyx,*
*I'm sorry for what I did.*
*Good luck at State.*
*Pepper*

I look up at Peter.

"You know how she is." He shrugs. "She was supposed to go talk to Coach, tell her what happened, and offer to do restitution so she can play at State. Instead, she quit the team. Now Dad's pissed, too. He says she threw away her shot at a scholarship, and she thinks it's everyone else's fault."

I lay the card back down on the bed. Then I look at him.

"I'm sorr—" His voice fades away. He shoves his hands in his coat pockets, turns toward the door, pauses, and leaves without saying goodbye.

## CHAPTER 41

# Coach Calls

"Alyx?" Mom suddenly appears, handing me the phone. "It's Coach."

"Yeah?" I sound like a droid.

Coach is all business. "Alyx, don't talk, listen. I spoke with Bender. Even though your doctor from California faxed the records, he's not backing down on the verification with a local physical. I want you to know I see this for what it is — utter nonsense and unacceptable discrimination. Your doctor has sent them everything they need. He even personally called, but Mr. Bender hasn't acquiesced yet." She's quiet for a moment. "This might come down to the wire. Either way, the team has reached consensus on this. We all support you. Unless everyone has the opportunity to play, none of us play, but I need to know if you think you'll be ready to play by Friday?"

"Pepper quit?" I cough.

Coach is quiet on the other end. I imagine her fiddling with her silver whistle. "Her father turned in her uniform yesterday."

I swallow hard. A wet sound rumbles into the phone. "Maybe," I whisper.

Not exactly an answer, but Coach says, "Good, rest up. I'll call tomorrow."

I hand the phone back to Mom. "Pepper quit."

I should feel like celebrating, but for some reason all I feel is pissed off.

Mom sets the phone on the tray with two cups half full of cold echinacea tea. Her forehead furrows. "Quit?"

I nod, staring at the butterfly card lying on the quilt.

Mom picks up the tray, balancing it against her hip with one arm. "She was behind all this, wasn't she?"

I shrug, then stare at the ugly bottom feeder fish that is using its mouth to crawl up the side of the tank. Q fish is doing laps, avoiding its tentacles.

Mom presses her lips together. "Alyx, it's better to talk about this stuff." She sits at the end of my bed, shifting the tray on her knees. "It seems to me that Pepper wanted to go to State more than any girl on that team, so why would she quit now?"

I can't answer that. I look out the window toward the park. The snow has been cleared away under the basket closest to Pepper's house. But she's not out there. Except for one light upstairs, the rest of her house is dark.

"How about you?" Mom puts her hand on mine.

"Coach says it's either all of us or none of us."

Mom pats my hand, smiles, and stands up. "Good!" She heads for the door and with her free hand knocks a pair of dirty socks off the desktop. "Now, rest and get better."

By noon, Mom's left for work and my fever's broken and, even though he's been told not to, Grandpa sneaks in to check on me.

I lie in bed all afternoon, listening to the answering machine go *click-buzz, click-buzz, click-buzz.* Mom turned its voice recorder off. I run through our plays and wonder how they'll work without Pepper. Most of the points I've made all season came from working the boards. With Pepper gone, will Shana pass me the ball? Or refuse, like always?

At three in the afternoon, Mom pops her head in the door. "There's a bunch of messages on the machine."

I don't want to hear them.

"Your first game is scheduled for six on Friday. Against West. Let's just count on Mr. Bender coming around. Do you think you can do it?" I feel my braces rubbing against the inside of my cheeks as I unconsciously clench my jaw, hesitate, and finally nod. I hear her making hotel reservations in Madison.

CHAPTER 42

# Pit Stop

Friday morning rolls around quickly. Coach calls and says Bender isn't budging. It's possible we'll get all the way to Madison and not get to play, but we're going anyway.

Mom disappears down the stairs to the basement and returns shortly after. She pulls a cup and saucer from the cabinet and pours steaming black coffee from the pot. Her bare feet squeak against the linoleum floor.

"Your grandpa's under the weather."

I scrape up the remainder of my oatmeal. "Is he sick?"

"I think he's got what you had. He probably won't make it to the game today, Honey. But he wants to talk to you before you leave."

"Okay." I swallow the last bite of oatmeal, feeling incredibly guilty that I've gotten him sick.

Mom sits across from me and takes a long sip from her cup. I stare out the window as she studies my face.

Soon, Grizzly pants up the steps. Mom motions that we should follow him back down. Grandpa's propped up on the bed with his hooked-rug pillows. He squints at me, his glasses resting on the bedside table.

Past the window, exhaust billows from the bus that Grizzly's warming up.

"Heard you gotta go up against our crosstown rivals right outta the box."

I nod.

"Damn good team. Heard they were outplaying the Bulldogs by the end of the season. So, you take that first game and you'll clinch the whole tourney. Whaddaya think?"

"Maybe so," I respond.

His eyes look smaller, cloudier, without his glasses on. When he reaches out his hand, it's shaking. I step closer and take his hand in mine.

"You stick close to your uncle, you hear? That's what we Kowalskis do when times get tough. You can't do this alone, kid. No one expects you to."

My eyes start to water.

Grizzly pulls up his sleeve and flexes his muscle. His bicep bulges. "Don't nobody mess with Joey Kowalski and live to tell about it!"

Mom laughs. I smile. Grizzly presses his arms together in an Arnold Schwarzenegger pose. Grandpa squeezes my hand weakly and then releases it.

"Go on," he motions us to the door. "I'll be fine."

When we pull up to Cudahy High, the entire team, minus Pepper, streams out the front door with their bags and shoes dangling from their shoulders. MJ leaps on the bus first, catches sight of me, and yells, "She's here!" Then she dashes down the aisle and slides in next to me, throwing her arms around me. "I told 'em you'd come."

I stiffen, even though it feels good to be back with the team. Mary and Martha are next on the bus.

"Alyx! Thank God!" They give me high fives as they file past. Roslyn's face lights up when she walks down the aisle. She takes the seat directly behind MJ and me and gives me a pat on the back.

I see Coach standing outside the bus talking with Grizzly. Her face looks serious. Holding a phone, she steps away from the bus. Grizzly uses his body to block the wind for her. When she's finished, they climb on and she holds up a hand.

Someone pops a gum bubble behind me.

"Okay, ladies. This is what we've worked for." She looks directly at me. "Alyx, we're glad you're here."

"Hallelujah," MJ whispers, elbowing me. A murmur moves through the bus. Roslyn pats my shoulder again. I cough to keep from tearing up.

Coach continues, "Cammy's here to help us in the forward position."

There's a polite applause for the girl from the JV team. Shana, who's the one chomping gum, calls out, "We can't replace Pepper."

Quiet conversation breaks out all over the bus.

"Pepper's the one who quit," Mary says, and Martha adds, "Yeah, she hung herself!"

Coach puts up her hand. "I just got off the phone. Pepper's father and I agree that if a few apologies come first," she zeros in on Martha, "from both sides of this, then Pepper will be allowed to play, but this needs to be a team decision."

I slump in my seat. MJ puts her hand on my knee. I feel numb. There's a few groans.

"After what she did to Alyx!" Martha jumps up and Mary quickly joins her, "Yeah, we can win without her! Why should we have to apologize to her?"

Shana whips around. "Oh? Let's see. You only tweeted a million messages about what a narcissistic, Mafia-princess, schizophrenic, bipolar bitch she is!"

The bus breaks out in pandemonium. Everyone's pointing fingers. Arguing. Stephanie and MJ are going at it right next to me.

*She said, I said, she said . . .*

Coach walks down the aisle, looking at us, until one by one, everyone shuts up.

"No one here today is privy to all the facts, including me. Though the inaccurate and hurtful messages circulating over the last week have not helped anything, it'll be better to handle this as a team and in person, so we'll be at Pepper's house in five minutes. But this has to be a team decision."

My stomach begins to churn. I stare blankly at the graffiti etched on the seat in front of me. Underneath POLLOCK'S SUCK, someone's written, FUCKING QUEERS QUIT VANDALIZING THIS BUS!

Coach's words skim over my head: "This is your team, girls. Decide amongst yourselves how you collectively want to handle this." She sits down.

*Apologize to Pepper? What for?*

Stephanie hollers, "Okay, hey, I have an idea!"

All the girls turn to look at her.

"When we get to to Pepper's house, MJ and I'll go in first."

Shana hops to her feet. "No! It's gotta be all of us, together. Including him-her-it." She points at me, disgusted.

"God, Shana!" Martha whacks Shana's head with her shoe.

"Whatever. I'm just sayin' that Pepper won't come if she thinks we hate her, and you guys were friggin' ruthless."

MJ presses her lips together. "Like Pepper's sooo sensitive."

Shana retorts with a fake laugh, then flips MJ off, which Coach doesn't see.

I sink down, wishing I could just disappear. I can't believe this is happening, and a part of me can't help but think whatever they said about Pepper, no matter how inaccurate, it couldn't have been mean enough. But at least they all now know the truth.

Roslyn places her hand on my shoulder as Grizzly steers the bus into the Pitmanis' driveway. She's been unusually quiet.

I try not to think about what they all think of me. But, in some weird way, I feel freer than I've ever felt. In. My. Entire. Life.

When the bus stops, Stephanie leaps up. "Let's go."

The entire team, including Coach, files out of the bus, but my legs refuse to budge. Coach shades her eyes and looks back at the bus. I slide out of sight, but keep watching over the edge of the seat.

The front door opens and Mr. Pitmani's bulky frame darkens the doorway. His head moves back and forth adamantly. Suddenly, in the window above him, the curtain moves.

It's Pepper.

She sees me.

I see her.

She disappears. Directly below her, the door closes, everyone turns, and they pile back onto the bus.

Coach says to Grizzly, "No go."

Voices buzz around me.

Coach blows her whistle. The shrill sound silences the bus. "Okay, girls. Save your energy."

Grizzly cranks the ignition. It whines, dies. He tries again. Same thing happens.

"Oh, sweet Jesus." MJ leans her head on my shoulder like she's swooning and everyone laughs, except me, because my eyes are glued to Pepper's window.

Grizzly pops the hood and Coach follows him out of the bus.

Pepper's head appears between the curtains again. No one notices, except me.

I can tell she's been crying and, in that moment, I feel closer to Pepper than ever before. The whole team must have really ganged up on her. They must have said stuff that really got to her. There's no other way she'd be missing the Championship if that weren't the case.

Now, she's the one who's lost all her friends. Her team.

Grizzly motions Coach into the driver's seat, his head's under the hood. The girls who have exited the bus crowd around him and cheer when it rumbles back to life.

I watch Pepper, who is still in the window.

Then I stare at the word *queer* on the seat in front of me. Aren't we all queer? Different? Odd? Peculiar? Strange? Freaky? Weird? Losers in our own way?

Grizzly's the last one to lumber back on the bus. He squeezes back into the driver's seat and flips the door shut. He shifts into gear and begins to reverse the bus.

"Uncle Joe, *stop!*" I hear myself yell. He hits the breaks. I jump over MJ and race toward the front of the bus.

"I need to talk to her," I explain.

He looks at me, nods at Coach, and flips the door open.

"What the hell's she doing?" I hear Shana say.

I run up to the door, and Peter opens it just as my foot hits the step. It's almost like he's expecting me, but I race past him into the hallway beyond the foyer. The house still smells of leather, stale beer, and musty old books.

"Where's Pepper's room?" I pant.

He points in astonishment at the curved stairwell. "First door on the left."

I bound up the steps two at time.

Pepper's door is ajar. She's lying on the floor beneath the window dressed in a new uniform and our team sweats. Her face is streaked with tears.

When I say her name, she lifts her head and snarls, "Who let you in?"

My hands are balled into sweaty fists.

"I already told 'em forget it!" she yells.

I hear footsteps in the foyer. She jumps to her feet and storms toward me, but I stand in the doorway blocking her exit, forcing her to either run me over or to stop.

She stops.

Right in front of my face.

"Get out of my room, hermaphrodyke!" Spit flies from her mouth. Our noses almost touch. I'm not afraid, and I should hate her, but I don't.

"We need you," is all I say.

And that's when I realize Pepper hates herself even more than she hates me. I feel it, and I feel sorry for her. I stare back, smiling when I say, "There's no 'I' in the word team, but there is in hermaphrodite, h-e-r-m-a-p-h-r-o-d-i-t-e!" And it's a real smile, and it doesn't hurt.

Pepper pushes past me, crying, saying to Peter, "She's the liar! Not me! Why does everybody hate *me* for telling the truth?"

I turn around just as Mr. Pitmani steps up behind Peter.

"Patti, calm down." His voice is surprisingly calm. Gentle. "No one hates you."

Pepper gulps in a breath and covers her face with her hands. "They do, and now you hate me, too!"

Mr. Pitmani walks to her side. He awkwardly puts his arms around her and whispers something in her ear. Pepper points at me, and whimpers, "She's the one who lied. She tricked me—she tricked all of us. She's the one who ruined the season, not me. She's the one who should say she's sorry."

Mr. Pitmani glances at me. "No, I'm the one who's sorry. If I'd have kept things in perspective, I wouldn't have pushed you so hard, and maybe none of this would've happened."

Pepper's hands drop. She looks at her dad in astonishment. "But she lied. Like Mom—"

He shakes his head. "Being truthful with someone isn't the same as disclosing private matters. And your mother, well," he glances at Peter, "your brother's helped me see I had a role to play in that whole situation."

Pepper looks confused. "But—"

Mr. Pitmani looks like he's about to cry. "Patti, I said in anger that you're your mother's girl, but you're not. You're *my* girl, and I'm sorry for having been so hard on you."

"You don't hate me?" She looks at her dad. Her face is streaked with tears.

He takes her by the shoulders. "I don't approve of everything you did, but no, I don't hate you, and I don't blame you. If I'd been around more, instead of sponging my brain in beer, none of this would have happened, and I don't want you to inherit my temper, either. I realize now that if you're going to be like me, I want it to be the good part of me." He pulls her into a hug. "That means we'll both go in and see Doc Evers when you get back. And you've got to promise to take your medication. Deal?"

Outside, a horn beeps and Peter grabs Pepper's gym bag. "Your team needs you!" He smiles at me. "Right, Alyx?"

Mr. Pitmani releases Pepper and nods his head in approval.

The horn beeps again.

Pepper looks like she's in shock.

I look at Peter, who looks at Mr. Pitmani, then I turn to Pepper. "We can win if you join us."

"You can! Bring home that cup." Peter grabs us each by an arm and drags us out to the bus.

A series of hoots and whistles ring out from the bus. Grizzly beeps the bus horn.

Peter pushes us into the bus. "I don't know exactly what you are, Alyx," his breath smells like spearmint, "but you rock!"

"Let's get this show on the road!" Coach hollers. She's smiling, cradling the phone to her ear again. She clicks it off and waves us on.

Pepper stops on the top step as though she's afraid. Coach motions her in and then holds up her hand. Everyone quiets down.

"Girls, good news, I just received word. We will be allowed to play tonight as scheduled!"

The bus vibrates with claps, cheers, and shouts. MJ stands up and hollers, "NEW GAME!"

Everyone begins to chant: "NEW GAME! NEW GAME! NEW GAME!"

Pepper's face softens. MJ gets up and makes her way down the aisle toward Pepper. "So, hot head, did motormouth Alyx change your mind, or what?"

It's quiet for a moment, then everyone laughs and the edges of Pepper's mouth actually bend into a smile. She looks directly at me, her eyes filled with a kind of unspoken apology. And something more—like gratitude; maybe even a little admiration mixed in.

Maybe.

"Hey, you know Alyx," Pepper jokes back, "always talking up a blue streak. A person can hardly shut her up. And . . . well, my brain doesn't always work the way I want it to."

"Well, thank God you finally came to your senses girrrl!" MJ calls out. Then everyone starts laughing and singing and talking all at once.

I catch Grizzly's eyes reflecting in the rearview mirror. He winks and I flash him a thumbs-up back.

## CHAPTER 43

# Mad Town

We make it to Madison in record time. The narrow streets su rounding the Capitol are crowded with a kaleidoscope of people, school colors, team jackets, and custom-made State-bound T-shirts.

Grizzly seems to know his way around the city's small, one-way streets. He steers the bus right through the university campus, passing dozens of fraternity and sorority houses along the lake. Bundled up students spill off every curb, walking, running, even biking, as they dodge in and out of traffic. When the bus pulls up in front of Camp Randall Stadium, there's already a long line of buses parked along the street. Girls from all over Wisconsin are lugging mesh bags full of basketballs, gym bags, and high-top tennis shoes.

I spot the Sunbug parked on the opposite side of the street where Mom's feeding a meter. There's a cop directing traffic at the intersection. The air smells like beer-soaked bratwurst.

Grizzly honks at Mom and she waves.

Everyone on the bus gets quiet. Most of us have never seen Madison before. Months earlier, throngs of protestors had filled the streets chanting and singing in objection to the governor's attempt to take collective bargaining rights away from teachers. Grizzly said it reminded him of what it was like in the sixties; only this time, the crowds were pushing baby carriages not dope.

Once we're stopped, Coach stands up. She turns and looks up and down the aisle at us. Everyone except Pepper is watching her, waiting. Pepper's eyes are closed. I can tell she's pretending to sleep.

I keep remembering her face when she was talking to her dad. She looked so scared.

Coach starts, "Girls—" but her voice catches, and she wipes at her eyes, lifting the silver whistle in her mouth and giving it a soft toot, motioning us to follow her.

Grizzly flips the door open. Cold air blows into the bus.

Pepper opens her eyes and follows Martha, who files out of the bus ahead of us.

Roslyn waits for me to pass. She taps my butt lightly, keeping her voice low, "Alyx, it's true, what Peter said. You rock."

I smile. Even though I'm not much of a believer, it feels like a miracle we're even here. And it feels good, knowing that none of the girls hate me. Not even Pepper—at least not anymore. But I can't help think that, maybe, it would've been better if I'd told them all the truth before—about who I really am.

Roslyn gives me a gentle shove from behind, resting her hands on my shoulders and giving them a little squeeze. The warmth of her hands feels good, but I don't turn around.

"Hurry up, your awesomeness!" she teases.

I smile, running my tongue over my braces, which come off next week. I'm starting to feel a little less freaky more and more, a little more myself, almost normal. Unconsciously, my body starts to shift into gear, and I'm ready to play, run, jump, shoot. My body's ready to do the one thing it could always get right.

"Come on, team!" Coach waves us off the bus.

"Gooo Cougars!" I hear Grizzly doing the Cudahy Cougar growl behind us.

## CHAPTER 44

# Plan B, Play B, Deuce It!

Coach's face is dead serious as we step off the court in the second overtime of the championship game. She motions for us to sit. My legs are like rubber. Roslyn hands me a water bottle and rubs my sweaty shoulders. My stomach's in knots. I take long, slow breaths.

The Lady Cougars and the defending champions, the Washington Bulldogs, are the only two teams that have proved unstoppable.

Until now.

Coach thought we were going to have to beat the Bulldogs right out of the box, but as it turned out, it was our long-time rivals, West, we tromped first, and now, finally, in the last tournament game, we're tied with the Bulldogs, 47–47, with thirty seconds left on the clock.

"Alyx, stay with Toya. Pepper, cover the middle." Coach looks at the clock as she barks orders. "Full-court press. I want all of you in their faces. Don't let them shoot!"

Mary, who's nursing a sprained ankle, hands MJ a paper bag. MJ waves it away. She's already puked her guts out. It's so loud that even with Coach yelling, we barely hear her. Unable to keep focused, my eyes scan the crowd, and I spot Peter crouched down under our basket, a video camera in his hand, and the manual camera he showed me the night of the dance hanging by a strap around his neck. He sees me, shrugs his shoulders, and smiles.

I shake my head, but smile back. And suddenly, I feel cool as a cucumber, even though I don't know what's going to happen with him or me or this game.

When the buzzer sounds, we race back out onto the court, trying to look light on our feet. I find Toya, positioning myself between her and the basket. She smells of sweat and coconut oil.

I look back to make sure Pepper's got the middle.

She sees me. Nods. Her eyes are two steel ball bearings glinting back at me. I can almost hear her thinking: *Pitmanis never lose!* Throughout the tournament, her shot's been off, but instead of getting pissed, she's been funneling the ball to me, or MJ, who's our lead scorer for this game.

Toya grunts, jabs with her elbow, and tries to ditch me as the Bulldogs snap the ball back into play. They pass the ball like a rapid-fire gun, forcing our guards to lurch and lunge for it.

The entire auditorium counts down with the clock. "Fifteen. Fourteen. Thirteen . . ."

Suddenly, Stephanie knocks away a pass, but she can't grab the ball. It bounces down the court, both teams scrambling, tripping, and leaping over one another to get it.

I stick to Toya like glue—like Coach asked—but out of the corner of my eye, I see Pepper leave her post to dive on top of the pile. Unbelievably, she emerges from the mess dribbling the ball, blood dripping from her nose.

"Nine. Eight. Seven . . ." the crowd chants.

Immediately, Pepper's swarmed by Bulldogs, but before the ref can call a foul, the ball's batted away. It rolls in front of Toya, but I'm faster. I grab it, look down the court, and see that no one is open, except Pepper, who sees me and breaks free from the swarm of Bulldogs.

She looks at the clock, back at me, her face rigid with panic. For a split second, I'm not sure what to do. I'm not even sure I'm looking at the right basket. Then, it's like everything goes into slow motion, my body takes over, and I remember the dream with Dad and "Plan B." I hold up two fingers and race by Pepper, drawing the entire Bulldog team after me.

"Deuce!" I holler as I whip by.

"Six. Five. Four . . ."

Pepper mouths, "No!" I can see she thinks I've lost my mind. I hear her feet slap the floor behind me and I hear her panting, trying to keep pace.

"Alyx, what the hell?"

And then it's too late to stop. I lay the ball up lightly as a pile of Bulldogs crash down on me.

"Three. Two—" the buzzer blares, and beneath the crush of bodies I hear, "Basket goooooooood!"

Dozens of flashes go off, the light blinding me. Above the roar, I hear the rapid-fire click of Peter's new camera and Pepper, somewhere on the pile of bodies, swearing and crying at the same time. "Why'd you do that, Alyx? I could have missed."

Crawling out of the pile on all fours, I start to laugh. Still blinded, trying to get back on my feet, I holler back, "I knew you wouldn't!"

And then, before I can get up, Pepper flies from the pile and tackles me, laying me out flat on my back. She's got me pinned down like we're in a wrestling match. Her face is smeared with sweat, blood, and tears, and her eyes are fierce, some expression I can't decipher.

"What?" I say, looking up at her. "You won the game."

"No," she shakes her head, and starts to stand up. "We did."

## CHAPTER 45

# The Right Move

As we pull onto the Harbor Street Bridge, I look out over Milwaukee's southside and lean my cheek against the frosty bus window. I've gotten used to the malty, yeasty smell of Milwaukee's air. Behind a thin, misty wall of fog blowing in off Lake Michigan, I see the outline of the Polish Palace. It looks so small from here.

I check my phone and see that I finally got an email from Dylan. At the end of the school year, he's flying from Ecuador to Chicago, because, like MJ, he got into the UW and wants to check it out and visit me. I close my eyes and listen to the chorus of girls' voices around me. I imagine Grandpa resting, waiting at home in a sea of hooked rugs. And Mom, who's probably already beaten us home in the Sunbug—maybe at this very moment, she's fixing Grandpa's favorite dinner, Polish sausage with sauerkraut.

And Dad? I think about him, too. I hear his voice whispering, "Plan B." Then it occurs to me that, like

Mr. Pitmani, maybe Dad did really love me; he just had a hard time saying it.

I hear Grizzly laughing in the front of the bus. He and MJ are leading everyone in a medley of rap songs. Most of the team is crowded in the front of the bus. Except for Roslyn. Pepper's leaning against her, fast asleep for real this time, her arms wrapped around the Gold trophy cup in her lap. Roslyn smiles, then winks at me. It's obvious she's not going to move until Pepper wakes up. I smile back, grateful—and not a bit worried—that she's my friend.

On the back of the seat in front of me, someone's carved a word right into the metal. It shines up at me. Unable to stop smiling, I trace my finger over it.

*Queer.*

From the *Milwaukee Journal Sentinel*:

## COUGAR GIRLS TAKE STATE!

*In a nail-biting final tournament game, the Cudahy Cougars hit the floor with last year's State Champs, the Washington Bulldogs. Two overtimes and mounting foul trouble on both sides sent key players to the bench, including the Cougar's center, six-foot sophomore, Alyx Kowalski, whose gender was brought into question just days before the tournament. However, she was granted eligibility only hours before the games commenced.*

*In the second overtime, with Kowalski on the bench, Washington Bulldog Toya Woods towered over the center* lane, and the Cougars lost their edge. With only a minute on the clock, Cougar point guard, Stephanie Wexler, hit a key three-point basket, tying the score for the third time.

The Bulldogs tried to rally as the clock wound down, but after a series of timeouts and scrambles, with both teams having trouble hanging onto the ball, Coach Chance put Kowalski back in the game. With three seconds on the clock, Kowalski managed to grab the ball. Flashing a peace sign, she took off down the court, tipping the ball off the boards to senior Patti (Pepper) Pitmani, who sank the game-winning shot as the buzzer blasted.

This game marked the first time in twenty-three years that the Cudahy Cougars have traveled to the state tournament. This is their first Big Cup.

Coach Carol Chance's record stands for itself, though she says, "The credit goes to the girls. They pulled together and played like a team." When asked if the eligibility of Kowalski made a difference in the outcome of the tournament, she flashed us a smile along with the now famous Cudahy Cougar peace sign, which we're told stands for a play called Deuce.

# Acknowledgments

I am deeply grateful to the many people who have helped make this book a reality—my son Quinn Schwellinger, my partner Roseann Sheridan, and all my friends at Vermont College, an amazing array of talented writers, especially Tobin (MT) Anderson, Tim Wynne-Jones, Alison McGhee, and Liza Ketchum, who may never know how much their early encouragement meant; as well as Marion Dane Bauer for her unwavering faith in my writing and this book.

Other authors who helped in both large and small ways to make this book possible include Nancy Garden, Susa Silvermarie, Kathi Appelt, Alex Sanchez, Kevin Henkes, Jane Hamilton, and David Rhodes. My amazing writing group: Gayle Rosengren, Jacqueline Houtman, Amy Laundrie, Amanda Bosky, Jennifer Reinfeld, Cindy Schumerth, and Lisl Detlefsen. Darlene Chandler Bassett, Mary Johnson, and all the audacious women of AROHO, my Lamba literary fellows and my dear friends, writers and non-writers alike: Kelly O'Ferrell, Janice Durand, Jean Allen, Leah Creswell, Sarah Williams, and Pamela Johnson. The great editors in my life: Kristen Jacobson, Lissa McGlaughlin, and of course, the remarkable Julie Matysik, and my agent, Jonathan Lyons—two extraordinary people with unparalleled skill and vision.

Finally, all those who are too numerous to name, including those who've shared your personal stories with me, my extended family members, the good folks who reside in Milwaukee's South Side, and the Intersex Society of North America.